Albert F. Blaisdell

Stories of the Civil War

adapted for supplementary reading

Albert F. Blaisdell

Stories of the Civil War
adapted for supplementary reading

ISBN/EAN: 9783337220990

Printed in Europe, USA, Canada, Australia, Japan

Cover: Foto ©Andreas Hilbeck / pixelio.de

More available books at **www.hansebooks.com**

STORIES

OF

THE CIVIL WAR

ADAPTED FOR

SUPPLEMENTARY READING

BY

ALBERT F. BLAISDELL

AUTHOR OF "THE STUDY OF THE ENGLISH CLASSICS," "CHILD'S BOOK OF
HEALTH," "HOW TO KEEP WELL," "OUR BODIES AND HOW WE
LIVE," "FIRST STEPS WITH AMERICAN AND ENGLISH
AUTHORS," "READINGS FROM THE
WAVERLEY NOVELS," ETC.

BOSTON MDCCCXCIII
LEE AND SHEPARD PUBLISHERS
10 MILK STREET NEXT "THE OLD SOUTH MEETING HOUSE"

STORIES OF THE CIVIL WAR.

PREFACE

Tʜɪꜱ is a book of stories about the Civil War. It is not a history — only a book of stories edited for school and home use. Our aim has not been to crowd the mind with facts, but to arouse in the younger generation a lively interest in the brave men who fought in the war for the Union.

We have tried to present a series of pictures of our national life during the late war, around which a fuller knowledge of the course of its history may gather.

These stories are designed to interest as well as to instruct young people, and to excite in their minds a keen desire to know more of the noble deeds of their fathers and grandfathers, who sacrificed so much during this momentous period of our country's history.

In making selections from the great mass of books

about the war, we have kept in mind these three points:

First, to make such selections as are interesting, graphic, and founded on fact.

Second, to select those written by men who personally took part in the scenes which they describe.

Third, to prepare such pieces as will arouse a greater love and reverence for those who fought, bled, and died, that we, as a people, might live to-day in peace and prosperity.

The stories are written in a lively and attractive style, and in very simple language. In many of them a graphic style and terse diction will more than make up for any lack of rhetorical finish.

The thanks of the editor are due to Messrs. D. Appleton & Co. ; Fords, Howard, & Hulbert ; T. Y. Crowell & Co. ; Charles L. Webster & Co. ; and to the Publishers of the Youth's Companion, for kind permission to use selections from their copyrighted authors.

ALBERT F. BLAISDELL.

July, 1890.

CONTENTS

6 CONTENTS

STORIES OF THE CIVIL WAR

I

THE NATION'S PERIL

THIRTY years ago there took place, in this country, one of the most exciting political campaigns in American history. Abraham Lincoln, the candidate of the Republican party, was elected President of the United States on November 6, 1860.

A large book would not suffice to give the young student the full history of this campaign and the memorable events which followed during the next six months. It was the culmination of affairs which had taken place during the half-century before. It was the outburst of a storm which had been brewing for many long years. Wise statesmen of a former generation had foreseen, with mingled sorrow and dismay, just such a crisis in our country's history. The deep-seated cause, of which a long and costly war was the natural result, is a subject for earnest study in connection with the formal history of the United States. It does not come within the scope of this book.

As soon as the election of Lincoln was announced, men of extreme views at the South proceeded at once to carry out their threats of attempting to withdraw from the Union. Seven States seceded, at intervals more or less brief, from the Union, and organized what was known as the Southern Confederacy. Four States seceded later. The people at the North were amazed at the rapidity with which the organization against the national government established itself. The humiliating events of that dread winter of 1860–61 are a part of our history. The government at Washington stood as if paralyzed. The President was a weak, old man, and did not know what to do. Most of his cabinet officers were friendly to the South, and took advantage of their official positions to allow the enemies of the country to take possession of the national stores, arms, arsenals, forts, and navy yards, within the limits of the seceding States. The government did not even dare to send re-enforcements to the forts along the southern seacoast lest such action should precipitate a civil war. This weak and irresolute action gave the seceding States ample opportunity to prepare for the coming strife at the expense of the nation. This cost the country many millions of dollars and thousands of lives to regain during the next four years.

Such, briefly, was the condition of the country when Abraham Lincoln, fearful of life, came to Washington in March, 1861, and quietly took the reins of the government. How little could the good President, or even the wisest of his advisers, realize the overwhelming responsibility of his position.

With the stirring events which followed we are familiar. The story of how Major Anderson removed his little band of United States troops from Fort Moultrie to Fort Sumter, in Charleston harbor, for greater safety, is a familiar one; likewise, how the Confederates fired upon a vessel sent with supplies intended for it; and, finally, after a severe bombardment, how they compelled the fort to surrender. Forbearance had ceased to be a virtue. It was seen even by the most timid and conservative that something must be done at once to assert the majesty and power of the national government. President Lincoln acted resolutely and promptly. On the 15th of April, 1861, he issued a proclamation calling out seventy-five thousand militia, for three months, to suppress the rebellion.

The people of the North answered promptly and vigorously to the dry and formal words of the proclamation. No one had suspected how deep in the hearts of the people was the sentiment of patriotism. The lowering of the flag at Fort Sumter pierced the pride and the honor of the North to the quick. The morning and evening of a single day saw peace utterly laid aside, and twenty millions of people filled with the spirit of war.

The same scenes were at the same time occurring in the Southern States. Even more fiery was the outbreak, because the people were of more demonstrative natures.

And thus it came to pass that thirty millions of people, divided into two bands, went seeking each other through the darkness and mystery of war.

II

THE BOMBARDMENT OF FORT SUMTER

[*The Story as told by an Eye-witness.*]

IT was already near morning (April 12, 1861). The east was changing, and a faint twilight came stealing over the harbor (Charleston), every moment growing brighter. At no moment of the day has light such an enchanting effect as between twilight and sunrise. Everything has a freshness, an unworn and pure look, as if it had just been created. A light film of mist lay along the rim of the harbor; but within that silver setting the water lay dark and palpitating. Out of its bosom rose Fort Sumter, sheer from the water, which lapped its very base on every side. How serene and secure the fort looked! How beautifully the morning brightened around it, though as yet the sun rose far down below the sea.

I was startled by the roar of a mortar a little behind me. Out of its white smoke rose, with graceful curve, a bomb that hurtled through the air and burst above the fort.

"May violence overtake the wretch, and a disgraceful death!" I did not know that it was my own State that broke the peace. Edmund Ruffin it was, an old man with white hair that hung down in profusion over his shoulders, and was now flying wild, his eyes bright with an excitement either of fanaticism or insanity.

This single shot given, there was a dead pause for a moment or two. A flock of wild ducks, startled from their feeding-ground, flew swiftly along the face of the water, and were lost behind the fort. The peace was gone. This tranquil harbor was changed to a volcano. Jetting forth from around its sides came tongues of fire, wrapped in smoke, and the air was streaked with missiles converging from every side and meeting at Sumter. Now that the circle was once on fire it flamed incessantly. Gun followed gun — battery answered battery — and the earth fairly trembled with the explosions. I was fascinated. I could not withdraw. I waited to see the fort deliver its fire. It stood silent.

As the sun flamed above the horizon and shot its light across the waters, up rose the flag from the fort, gracefully climbing to its topmost height, and rolled out its folds, as if it were sent up to look out over the troubled scene and command peace. Still no gun from the fort replied. Two hours of bombarding, and not a shot in return. But at seven in the morning, a roar from the lower tier of guns gave notice that the fort had roused itself and joined in the affray. Its shot ·began to fall around me. I retreated within the battery, and then, sick and heart-heavy, I determined to make my way back to the city. My heart was with the seventy men battling for the flag against five thousand.

As I drew near the city, I began to hear the church bells ringing wild with joy. Crowds everywhere lined the wharves, filled the streets, covered the roofs of the hitherward houses. The people had been out all night. Many, discouraged at the delay, had begun returning to their homes. But the first sound of a gun brought them back with alacrity. One would think that the humbling of the national flag was the most joyous occasion in the world.

All the afternoon the same continuous firing filled every part of the city with its sound. Volumes of black smoke rolled up from the fort. It was on fire. Its guns fired but infrequently. Every time the smoke rolled away I looked anxiously through the glass to see if the flag still waved. The sun went down upon ˙. All night, but at intervals of fifteen minutes, the bombardment went on. People who had expected to reduce

the fort in a few hours seemed discouraged at this pro-
tracted defence.

The morning came, and with its first full light the
forts that lay in a circle round the fort opened in order,
Johnson on the south, Cummings' Point on the east,
Moultrie on the north, and the floating battery on the
west, together with the smaller intermediate batteries.
As far as I could discern, the walls of Sumter had suffered little. No breach appeared. The barbette guns
were knocked away. But though they were the heavi-
est, they had never been used. The besiegers aimed to
sweep them with such a fire that the men could not
work them. Again the smoke rolled up from the fort,
and flames could now be seen. Moultrie poured a continuous stream of red-hot shot upon the devoted fort.
At last came noon. The firing ceased. Boats were
putting off to the fort. By one o'clock it was noised
abroad that the garrison had surrendered. It was true.
On Sunday noon, they were to salute the flag and evac-
uate the fort.

If the week days were jubilant, how shall I describe
the Sabbath? The churches were thronged with excited citizens. In many of these all restraint was
thrown off, and the thanksgiving and rejoicing for the
victory swept everything like summer winds. I went

to my own church.   The decorum of the service, which
is a bulwark against irreverent excitements, served, on
this occasion, a good purpose.   Yet, strange as it may
seem, in the lessons for the day occurred a passage that
sounded in my ears like a prophecy, and full of warning
and doom.   It was this: "Prepare war, wake up the
mighty men; let them come up.   Beat your plough-
shares into swords, and your pruning-hooks into spears ;
let the weak say, I am strong.   Multitudes, multitudes
in the valley of decision; for the day of the Lord is
near in the valley of decision."

As I came from church, a south wind blew, and I
heard the sound of cannon.   I walked rapidly to the
point, and only in time to see through my glass the flag
descending from over Sumter.   The drama is ended
— or rather opened! who can tell what shall be the end
of this?   It may be that all the roar and battle of the
two days past is as nothing to that which at some future
day shall precede the raising again of the flag over this
fallen fortress.   The future is in the hand of God.
Over the future hangs a dark cloud which I would that
I might pierce and know what it hides. .

III

SUNDAY IN NORWOOD AFTER THE FALL OF FORT SUMTER

[From Henry Ward Beecher's "Norwood."]

ON Sunday morning, the 14th of April, 1861, it was known that Fort Sumter had surrendered. The scales fell from men's eyes.

There was war !

The flag of the nation had been pierced by men who had been taught their fatal skill under its protection. The nation's pride, its love, its honor, suffered with that flag, and with it trailed in humiliation.

Without concert or council, the whole people rose suddenly with one indignation, to vindicate the nation's honor. It came as night comes, or the morning, broad as a hemisphere. It rose as the tides raise the whole ocean, along the whole continent, drawn upward by the whole heavens.

The frivolous became solemn ; the wild grew stern ; the young felt an instant manhood.

It was the strangest Sunday that ever dawned on

DEFENCE OF FORT SUMTER.

Norwood since the colonial days, when, by reason of
hostile Indians, the fathers repaired to church with
their muskets. All the region round came forth.
Never had such an audience gathered in that house.
Every face had in it a new life. Dr. Buell was not
wont to introduce into his Sabbath services topics allied
to politics, nor did he mean to change his habit to-day.

His sermon, weighty, and on themes which usually
are accounted more solemn than all others, yet sounded
light and empty in men's ears. Nor had he ever
preached with so much difficulty. He lost the connection, hurried passages which should have been deliberate, and afterwards owned that he was never so glad to
get through a sermon.

It was in the prayer following that the stream burst
forth. A mighty tide rose within him, and he poured
out his soul for the country. He prayed for the government, for the men in Fort Sumter, who had been
like the three children in the fiery furnace, for the flag,
and for all in authority, that they might have wisdom
and courage to vindicate it.

The house was still, so still that the ear ached between every pause. The word "Amen" set loose an
army of handkerchiefs, and people wiped more eyes
than were ever wet at once in that house. Just as Dr.

Buell rose to give out the closing hymn, he saw the choir rising as if to give an anthem. The minister sat right down ; but he quickly rose up again, and every man in the house, as the choir sang the "Star-Spangled Banner." Such a scene had never been known in sober Norwood. And when the last strain died, it was with difficulty that the minister could repress an open cheer.

"Why didn't you let 'em ? " said Deacon Marble. " It's enough to make the stones cry out. I never felt so sorry before that I hadn't a house full of boys."

Aunt Polly, for once, found nothing to rebuke in the deacon. "This is the Lord's work. Sunday isn't a bit too good to teach men that they ought 'er save the country ! . . . My gran'father dug the sile out from under this church to git saltpetre to make powder on, to fight for our liberties ! And I guess the old man's bones that's lyin' yonder shook when they heard them cannon jar ! Now's the time for folks to show themselves."

The whole population seemed to be in the street. Men formed groups and discussed the only topic. Party lines were fast rubbing out. There was an afternoon service, but it was like a dream. As yet men's feelings had found no channels, and no relief in action. A few discordant notes there were. Tough old

Hunt, farmer up in "Hardscrabble," as a poor neighborhood was called, in spite of angry eyes and frowning brows, would have his say : —

"I allus told you that the Abolitionists would bring blood on us. Now I hope they're satisfied. They've been teasin' and worryin' the South for twenty years, and now the South has turned and gored 'em. Sarved 'em right!"

"I tell ye, old leather-skin," said Hiram Beers, "you'd better shut up! The boys ain't in a temper to hear such talk. You'll git hurt afore you git through a hundred speeches like that."

Old Hunt was a small, wiry man, about sixty years of age, with black hair, and a turbid hazel eye that looked cruel when he was wrathful. Hiram's words set him aflame.

"Where's the man that's goin' to stop my tongue? This is a free country, I guess. I shall say what I've a mind to " —

Just then Hiram, who saw that trouble was brewing, changed the attack from the old man to his horse, who was as fiery and obstinate as his master, and already had exhausted his patience and fodder in a long Sunday under the horse-shed. While the old man was standing in his wagon, bristling all over like a black-

and-tan terrier, and fierce for opposition, Hiram gave his horse a keen cut where a horse least likes to be hit. The first thing Hunt knew, he was sprawling in his wagon, and the horse was heading for home with a speed unbecoming a Sabbath day. The old man, nimble and plucky, gathered himself up, utterly at a loss which he was most angry with, the public or the horse; now giving the animal a rousing pull, and then shaking his left fist back at the crowd, he disappeared from the green, in a medley of utterances which, addressed sometimes to his horse and sometimes to Hiram, and sometimes to the imaginary Abolitionists, formed a grotesque oration.

"I'm as much of a Democrat as he is," said Hiram, "and have allus gone with my party. But I tell ye, boys, this is no party matter. This is a black business, and there ain't but one way to settle it. We've tried the votes, and they won't stand that. Now we'll try the bullets, and the side that can stand that longest is goin' to rule this country, that's all."

Old Mr. Turfmould, the village undertaker, ventured to say, without meaning any harm — merely as a moral reflection :— "Ah, Mr. Beers, it's awful, killin' folks, and huddlin' 'em into holes without funerals and decent fixin's of any kind."

"Shet up, old owl!" said Hiram. "This thing's goin' to be fought out, that's sartain, and we won't have nobody hangin' back at home. A man that won't fight when his flag's fired on, ain't worth a dead nit."

Old Deacon Trowbridge was talking with Judge Bacon, to whom he usually deferred with profound respect for his legal learning.

"I hope," said Judge Bacon, with calm and gentle tones, "that the government will forbear and not be in haste to strike again. We ought not to think of coercion. Our Southern brethren will come to their reason if we are patient, and wait for their passions to subside."

"I tell ye, judge, we ain't goin' to wait. We've waited long enough, and this is what we've got for it! Secede! rob the government! shoot our flag! and kill our soldiers, shut up in the fort like chickens in a coop, and then not fight? You might as well have a Day of Judgment and nobody hurt. If we ain't goin' to fight now, we'd better swap clothes with the women, and let them try awhile. I tell ye we will fight!"

Deacon Trowbridge was like a green hickory fire on a winter's morning. It requires the utmost skill and blowing to get it to burn, but when once it is started, it blazes and crackles with immense heat, and speedily drives all those who were cuddling and shivering about it, far back into the room.

On he went, indignant at the judge, and talking to every one he met. "It's come! Ye can't help it. I don't want to help it! It's the Lord's will, and I am desperate willin'. If my boys — some on 'em — don't go, I'll disown 'em — don't want no cowards on my farm!"

The sun had gone down. Every household in Norwood and wide about was a scene of excitement. That night, prayer was a reality. Never before had the children heard from their fathers' lips such supplications for the country. Never before had the children's hearts been open to join so fervently in prayer themselves. Men seemed to be conscious that they were helpless in the presence of an immeasurable danger. By faith they laid their hearts upon the bosom of God, till they felt the beatings of that great Heart whose courses give life and law to the universe.

IV

BATTLE-HYMN OF THE REPUBLIC

[*By Mrs. Julia Ward Howe.*]

MINE eyes have seen the glory of the coming of the
Lord ;
He is trampling out the vintage where the grapes of
wrath are stored ;
He hath loosed the fateful lightning of his terrible
swift sword :
His truth is marching on.

I have seen him in the watchfires of a hundred cir-
cling camps ;
They have builded him an altar in the evening dews
and damps ;
I have read his righteous sentence by the dim and flar-
ing lamps :
His day is marching on.

I have read a fiery gospel writ in burnished rows of
steel :
"As ye deal with my contemners, so with you my grace
shall deal ;
Let the Hero, born of woman, crush the serpent with
his heel,
Since God is marching on."

He hath sounded forth the trumpet that shall never call
    retreat ;
He is sifting out the hearts of men before his judg-
    ment seat ;
Oh ! be swift, my soul, to answer him ! be jubilant, my
    feet !
            Our God is marching on.

In the beauty of the lilies Christ was born across the
    sea,
With a glory in his bosom that transfigures you and me ;
As he died to make men holy, let us die to make men
    free,
            While God is marching on.

V

THE DEATH OF COLONEL ELLSWORTH

IT was two o'clock on the morning of the twenty-fourth of May, 1861, when the expedition planned by General Scott started secretly from Washington to take military possession of Alexandria. One-half of the troops crossed the Long Bridge, and marched down the right bank of the Potomac, to enter Alexandria by the rear, and to cut off any Confederate troops who might be lurking about the city. The other half, including the Fire Zouaves under Colonel Ellsworth, went down the river in steamers, from the Washington Navy Yard. It was in the first gray of the morning, when the steamers touched at the wharves. Of this division Colonel Ellsworth was in command. He was one of the first to land. While the regiment was form-ing in line, one company was sent, post haste, to seize the telegraph station, that no communication could be sent to Richmond of their landing. This was of such vital importance that Colonel Ellsworth himself accompanied the party, passing through the streets on the full run.

On their way they went by the Marshall House, a hotel kept by one Jackson, over the roof of which a Confederate flag was flaunted. "We must have that flag," said Colonel Ellsworth, and, rushing in, he found a white man, in the front room, half dressed, and a negro. "Who raised that flag?" inquired the colonel. "I do not know," was the reply, "I am a boarder here." Followed by two or three, he sprang up-stairs to the roof of the house, seized the flag, and was descending with it in his hands, hardly a moment having been occupied in the movement, when the same half-dressed man, who had said that he was a boarder, but who proved to be Jackson himself, a brutal desperado, jumped from a dark passage, and, levelling a double-barrelled gun at Colonel Ellsworth's breast, at a distance of not more than two yards, fired a couple of slugs directly into his heart, and which, of course, proved fatal.

Ellsworth was on the second or third step from the landing, and he dropped forward with that heavy, horrible, headlong weight, which always comes of sudden death inflicted in such a manner. His assailant had turned like a flash to give the contents of the other barrel to Francis E. Brownell, a private, but either he could not command his aim, or the Zouave was too quick with him, for the slugs went over his head, and passed through the panels and wainscot of the door, which sheltered some sleeping lodgers. Simultaneously with his second shot, and sounding like the echo of the first, Brownell's rifle was heard, and the assassin staggered backward. His wound, exactly in the middle of the face, was frightful beyond description. Of course Brownell did not know how fatal his shot had been, and so, before the man dropped, he thrust his sabre bayonet through and through the body, the force of the blow sending the dead man violently down the upper section of the second flight of stairs.

The body of the murdered colonel was laid upon a bed; and the flag, stained with his blood, and purified by this contact from the baseness of its former meaning, was fitly laid about his feet.

Thus died, by the hand of a cowardly assassin, the brave and gallant Ellsworth. The tragic death of this young officer at a time when the country was not used to the horrors of war made a profound impression upon the people of the North.

VI

UNDER FIRE FOR THE FIRST TIME

How does a soldier feel who is under fire for the first time? To hear the bullets go singing past, now on this side, now on that, and now just overhead! How does a regiment act during its first battle? An officer of a Maine regiment thus vividly describes the behavior of his men during their first experience in battle. To one glancing along the line, the sight was ludicrous in the extreme. All were excited, and were loading and firing in every conceivable manner.

"Some were standing, but most were kneeling or lying down. Some were astride their pieces, and were ramming the charge totally regardless of the rules on that point. Many had poured their cartridges on the ground, and were 'peddling out' the lead with more speed than accuracy. We all took occasion to gibe our friends in gray to the best of our ability. So, with the din of musketry and the yells of friend and foe, it seemed as if bedlam were let loose.

"The behavior of those who were hit appeared most

singular ; and, as there were so many of them, it looked
as if we had a crowd of howling dervishes dancing and
kicking around in our ranks.

"A bullet often knocks over the man it hits, and rarely
fails by its force alone to disturb his equilibrium. Then
the shock, whether painful or not, causes a sudden
jump or shudder.

"Now, as every man, with hardly an exception, was
either killed, wounded, hit in the clothes, hit by spent
balls or stones, or jostled by his wounded comrades, it
follows that we had a wonderful exhibition. Some
reeled round and round, others threw up their arms
and fell over backward, others went plunging backward
trying to regain their balance ; a few fell to the front,
but generally the force of the bullet prevented this,
except where it struck low, and apparently knocked the
soldier's feet from under him. Many dropped the
musket and seized the wounded part with both hands,
and a very few fell dead.

"The enemy were armed with every kind of rifle and
musket, and as their front was three times ours, we
were under a cross-fire almost from the first. The
various tunes sung by the bullets we shall never forget,
and, furthermore, shall never confound them with any
we heard later. In a moment when curiosity got the

better of fear, I took notice of this fact, and made a
record of it in my diary a day or two afterward.

"The fierce *zip* of the minie bullets was not prominent by comparison at that particular moment, though
there were enough of them certainly. The main body
of sound was produced by the singing of slow, round
balls and buckshot fired from a smooth-bore, which do
not cut or tear the air as the creased ball does.

"Each bullet, according to its kind, size, rate of speed,
and nearness to the ear, made a different sound. They
seemed to be going past in sheets, all around and
above us."

When the war broke out, many officers on both sides,
even of high rank, were unskilled in military tactics.
Hence the art of war was rapidly learned, but at the
expense of stupid blunders and of many valuable lives.
A Confederate colonel gives the following interesting
sketch of his first battle. On entering a strip of wood,
it occurred to him that his men, being raw recruits,
would not fight well on horseback, and hence he ordered
them to dismount. This, of course, stopped the whole
body of the army behind the regiment. While the
men were leisurely tying their horses, an aide came up
at a furious gait and asked peremptorily : "What have
you stopped here for, and blocked up the whole road?"

UNDER FIRE FOR THE FIRST TIME.

" 'You mind your business,' said the adjutant ; 'our colonel knows what he's about.'

" I saw the point in a moment, and had them move out in the woods. In the meantime my scabbard got itself hitched in a tangled bush. So I told the battalion to form at the edge of the timber and wait for me. Then I cut the straps and left my broken scabbard in the bush, while, with naked blade flashing in my hand, I rushed to the front. Not a man could I find. They were anxious to see the fun, and had run over the brow of the hill, and scattered along the whole length of the line.

" With infinite difficulty I got them together, leaving wide gaps in the battle array. Barely in position, I heard a distant cannon, and at the same instant saw the ball high in the air. As near as I could calculate, it was going to strike about where I stood, and I dismounted with remarkable agility, only to see the missile of war pass sixty feet overhead.

" I felt rather foolish as I looked at my men, but a good deal relieved when I saw that they, too, had all squatted to the ground, and were none of them looking at me. I quickly mounted and ordered them to 'stand up.'

" We were soon ordered to charge, and drove the

enemy through the tall prairie grass, till they came to a creek and escaped. We passed some of the dead and wounded, the first sad results of real war that I had ever seen. At night the heavens opened wide, the rain fell in torrents; not even a campfire could be kept to light up the impenetrable gloom, and I sought a friendly mud-hole to sleep as best I could.

"The pale, rigid faces that I had seen turned up to the evening sun, appeared before me, as I tried in vain to shield my own from the driving rain, and as the big foot of a comrade, blundering round in the darkness, splashed my eyes full of mud, I closed them to sleep, muttering to myself: 'And this is war.'"

Here is a brave soldier's story of how he felt during his first battle.

"No person who was not upon the ground, and an eye-witness of the stirring scenes which there transpired, can begin to comprehend from a description the terrible realities of a battle; and even those who participated are competent to speak only of their own personal experience. Where friends and foes are falling by scores, and every species of missile is flying through the air, threatening each instant to send one into eternity, little time is afforded for more observation or reflection than is required for personal safety.

"The scene is one of the most exciting and exhilarating that can be conceived. Imagine a regiment passing you at 'double-quick,' the men cheering with enthusiasm, their teeth set, their eyes flashing, and the whole in a frenzy of resolution. You accompany them to the field. They halt. An aide-de-camp passes to or from the commanding general. The clear voices of officers ring along the line in tones of passionate eloquence. The word is given to march, and the body moves into action. For the first time in your life you listen to the whizzing of iron. Grape and canister fly into the ranks, bomb-shells burst overhead, and the fragments fly all around you. A friend falls; perhaps a dozen or twenty of your comrades lie wounded or dying at your feet; a strange, involuntary shrinking steals over you, which it is impossible to resist. You feel inclined neither to advance nor recede, but are spell-bound by the contending emotions of the moral and physical man. The cheek blanches, the lip quivers, and the eye almost hesitates to look upon the scene.

"In this attitude you may, perhaps, be ordered to stand an hour, inactive, havoc meanwhile marking its footsteps with blood on every side. Finally the order is given to advance, to fire, or to charge. And now, what a change! With your first shot you become a new man. Personal safety is your least concern. Fear has no existence in your bosom. Hesitation gives way to an uncontrollable desire to rush into the thickest of the fight. The dead and dying around you, if they receive a passing thought, only serve to stimulate you to revenge. You become cool and deliberate, and watch the effect of bullets, the shower of bursting shells, the passage of cannon-balls as they rake their murderous channels through your ranks, the plunging of wounded horses, the agonies of the dying, and the clash of contending arms, which follows the charge, with a feeling so calloused by surrounding circumstances that your soul seems dead to every sympathizing and selfish thought.

"Such is the spirit which carries the soldier through the field of battle. But when the excitement has passed, when the roll of musketry has ceased, the noisy voices of the cannons are stilled, the dusky pall of smoke has risen from the field, and you stroll over the theatre of carnage, hearing the groans of the wounded, discovering here, shattered almost beyond recognition, the form of some dear friend whom only an hour before you met in the full flush of life and happiness, — then you begin to realize the horrors of war, and experience a reaction of nature. The heart opens its floodgates, humanity asserts herself again, and you begin to feel.

"Friend and foe alike now receive your kindest services. The enemy, whom, but a short time before, full of hate, you were doing all in your power to kill, you now endeavor to save. You supply him with water to quench his thirst and with food to sustain his strength. All that is human or charitable in your nature now rises to the surface, and you are animated by that spirit of mercy which 'blesseth him that gives and him that takes.' A battle-field is eminently a place that tries men's souls."

VII

LITTLE EDDIE THE DRUMMER BOY

A FEW days before our regiment received orders to join General Lyon, on his march to Wilson's Creek, the drummer of our company was taken sick and conveyed to the hospital. On the night before the march, a negro was arrested within the lines of the camp, and brought before our captain, who asked him what business he had within the lines. He replied: "I know a drummer that you would like to enlist in your company, and I have come to tell you of it." He was immediately requested to inform the drummer that if he would enlist for our short term of service, he would be allowed extra pay, and to do this he must be on the ground early in the morning.

On the following morning there appeared before the captain's quarters during the beating of the *réveillé*, a middle-aged woman, dressed in deep mourning, leading by the hand a sharp, sprightly-looking boy, apparently about twelve or thirteen years of age. Her story was soon told. She was from East Tennessee, where her

husband had been killed by the Confederates and all
their property destroyed.

During the rehearsal of her story the little fellow
kept his eyes intently fixed upon the countenance of
the captain, who was about to express a determination
not to take so small a boy, when he spoke out : "Don't
be afraid, captain, I can drum." This was spoken with
so much confidence that the captain immediately observed, with a smile : "Well, well, sergeant, bring the
drum, and order our fifer to come forward." In a few
moments the drum was produced, and our fifer, a tall,
good-natured fellow, who stood, when erect, something
over six feet in height, soon made his appearance.

Upon being introduced to his new comrade, he
stooped down, with his hands resting upon his knees,
and, after peering into the little fellow's face a moment,
he observed: "My little man, can you drum?"—"Yes,
sir," he replied, "I drummed in Tennessee." Our fifer
immediately commenced straightening himself upward
until all the angles in his person had disappeared, when
he placed his fife at his mouth and played the " Flowers
of Edinborough," one of the most difficult things to follow
with the drum that could have been selected, and nobly
did the little fellow follow him, showing himself to be a
master of the drum. When the music ceased, our captain turned to the mother, and observed, —

"Madam, I will take your boy. What is his name?"

"Edward Lee," she replied; then, placing her hand upon the captain's arm, she continued, "Captain, if he is not killed" — here her maternal feelings overcame her utterance, and she bent down over her boy and kissed him upon the forehead. As she rose, she observed: "Captain, you will bring him back with you, won't you?"

"Yes, yes," he replied, "we will be certain to bring him back with us. We shall be discharged in six weeks."

An hour after, our company led the Iowa First out of camp, our drum and fife playing "The girl I left behind me." Eddie, as we called him, soon became a great favorite with all the men in the company. When any of the boys had returned from a foraging excursion, Eddie's share of the peaches and melons was the first apportioned out. During our heavy and fatiguing march, it was often amusing to see our long-legged fifer wading through the mud with our little drummer mounted upon his back, and always in that position when fording streams.

During the fight at Wilson's Creek, I was stationed with a part of our company on the right of Totten's battery, while the balance of our company, with a part

of an Illinois regiment, was ordered down into a deep
ravine upon our left, in which it was known a portion
of the enemy was concealed, with whom they were
soon engaged. The contest in the ravine continuing
some time, Totten suddenly wheeled his battery upon
the enemy in that quarter, when they soon retreated to
the high ground behind their lines. In less than
twenty minutes after Totten had driven the enemy
from the ravine, the word passed from man to man
throughout the army, "Lyon is killed!" and soon after,
hostilities having ceased upon both sides, the order
came for our main force to fall back upon Springfield,
while a part of the Iowa First and two companies of
the Missouri regiment were to camp upon the ground
and cover the retreat next morning. That night I was
detailed for guard duty, my turn of guard closing with
the morning call. When I went out with the officer as
a relief, I found that my post was upon a high eminence
that overlooked the deep ravine in which our men had
engaged the enemy, until Totten's battery came to
their assistance. It was a dreary, lonesome beat. The
moon had gone down in the early part of the night,
while the stars twinkled dimly through a hazy atmosphere, lighting up imperfectly the surrounding objects.
The hours passed slowly away, when at length the

morning light began to streak along the eastern sky, making surrounding objects more plainly visible. Presently I heard a drum beat up the morning call. At first I thought it came from the camp of the enemy across the creek ; but as I listened, I found that it came up from the deep ravine ; for a few minutes it was silent, and then I heard it again. I listened — the sound of the drum was familiar to me — and I knew that it was our drummer boy from Tennessee.

I was about to desert my post to go to his assistance, when I discovered the officer of the guard approaching with two men. We all listened to the sound, and were satisfied that it was Eddie's drum. I asked permission to go to his assistance. The officer hesitated, saying that the orders were to march in twenty minutes. I promised to be back in that time, and he consented. I immediately started down the hill through the thick undergrowth, and upon reaching the valley I followed the sound of the drum,. and soon found him, seated upon the ground, his back leaning against the trunk of a fallen tree, while his drum hung upon a bush in front of him, reaching nearly to the ground. As soon as he discovered me he dropped his drumsticks and exclaimed, "O corporal! I am so glad to see you. Give me a drink, please," reaching out his hand for my can-

teen, which was empty. I immediately turned to bring
him some water from the brook that I could hear rip-
pling through the bushes near by, when, thinking that
I was about to leave him, he began crying, saying:
"Don't leave me, corporal — I can't walk." I was
soon back with the water, when I discovered that he
was seriously wounded in both of his feet by a cannon-
ball. After satisfying his thirst, he looked up into my
face and said: "You don't think I will die, corporal, do
you? This man said I would not — he said the surgeon could cure my feet." I now discovered a man
lying on the grass near him. By his dress I recognized
him as belonging to the enemy. It appeared that he
had been shot through the bowels, and fallen near
where Eddie lay. Knowing that he could not live, and
seeing the condition of the boy, he had crawled to him,
taken off his buckskin suspenders, and corded the little
fellow's legs below the knee, and then lay down and
died. While he was telling me these particulars, I
heard the tramp of cavalry coming down the ravine,
and in a moment a scout of the enemy was upon us,
and I was taken prisoner. I requested the officer to
take Eddie up in front of him, and he did so, carrying
him with great tenderness and care. When we reached
the camp of the enemy, the little fellow was dead.

VIII

THE COMBAT BETWEEN THE MONITOR AND MERRIMAC

ABOUT nine o'clock on Saturday evening, March 8, 1862, Ericsson's new ironclad turret ship, the Monitor, reached Fortress Monroe from New York. Every exertion had been made by her inventor to get her out in time to meet the Merrimac; and the Confederates, finding out from their spies in New York that she would probably be ready, put a double force on their frigate and worked day and night. It is said that this extra labor gained that one day in which the Merrimac destroyed the Cumberland and the Congress.

The Monitor was commanded by Lieutenant John L. Worden. A dreadful passage of three days had almost worn out her crew. The sea had swept over her decks; the turret was often the only part above water. The tiller-rope was at one time thrown off the wheel. The draught-pipe had been choked by the pouring down of the waves. The men were half suffocated. The fires had been repeatedly extinguished. Ventilation had, however, been obtained through the turret. Throughout the preceding afternoon, Worden had heard the sound of the cannonading. He delayed but a few minutes at the fortress, and soon after midnight had anchored the Monitor alongside the Minnesota.

Day broke, a clear and beautiful Sunday. The flag of the Cumberland was still flying. The Merrimac approached to renew the attack. She ran down toward the fortress, and then came up the channel through which the Minnesota had passed. Worden at once took his station at the peep-hole of his pilot-house, laid the Monitor before her enemy, and gave the fire of his two eleven-inch guns. The shot of each was one hundred and sixty-eight pounds weight. Catesby Jones, who had taken command of the Merrimac, Buchanan having been wounded the day before, saw at once that he had on his hands a very different antagonist from those of yesterday. The turret was but a very small work to fire at, nine feet by twenty; the shot that struck it glanced off. One bolt only, from a rifle-gun, struck squarely, penetrating the iron. For the most part, the shots flew over the low deck, missing their aim.

Five times the Merrimac tried to run the Monitor down, and at each time received, at a few feet distance, the fire of the eleven-inch guns. In her movements, at one moment she got aground, and the light-drawing Monitor, steaming round her, tried at every promising point to get a shot into her. Her armor at last began to start and bend.

Unable to shake off the Monitor, or to do her any injury, the Merrimac now renewed her attack on the frigate Minnesota, receiving from her a whole broadside, which struck squarely. "It was enough," said the commander of the frigate, "to have blown out of the water any wooden ship in the world." In her turn, she sent from her rifled bow-gun a shell through the Minnesota's side; it exploded within her, tearing four of her rooms into one, and setting her on fire. Another shell burst the boiler of a tugboat which lay alongside the Minnesota. The frigate was firing on the ironclad solid shot as fast as she could.

Once more the Monitor ran between them, compelling her antagonist to change position, in doing which the Confederate ram again grounded, and again received a whole broadside from the Minnesota. The blows she was receiving were beginning to tell upon her. As soon as she could get clear, she ran down the bay, followed by the Monitor. Suddenly she turned round and attempted to run her tormentor down. Her beak grated on the Monitor's deck and was wrenched.

The turret ship stood unharmed a blow like that which had sent the Cumberland to the bottom; she merely glided out from under her antagonist, and in the act of so doing gave her a shot while almost in contact. It seemed to crush in her armor.

The Monitor now hauled off for the purpose of hoisting more shot into her turret. Catesby Jones thought he had silenced her, and that he might make another attempt on the Minnesota. He, however, changed his course as the Monitor steamed up, and it was seen that the Merrimac was sagging down at the stern. She made the best of her way back to Craney Island. The battle was over; the turreted Monitor had driven her from the field and won the victory.

The Minnesota had fired two hundred and forty-seven solid shot, two hundred and eighty-two shells, and more than ten tons of powder. The Monitor had fired forty-one shot, and was struck twenty-two times. The last shell fired by the Merrimac at her struck her pilot-house opposite the peep-hole, through which Worden at that moment was looking. He was knocked down senseless and blinded by the explosion. When consciousness returned, the first question this brave officer asked was: "Did we save the Minnesota?" The shattering of the pilot-house was the greatest injury that the Monitor received. On board the Merrimac two were killed and nineteen wounded. She had lost her iron prow, her starboard anchor, and all her boats ; her armor was dislocated and damaged ; she leaked considerably ; her steam-pipe and smoke-stack were riddled ; the muzzles of two of her guns were shot away ; the wood-work round one of the ports was set afire at every discharge.

This remarkable naval engagement excited the most profound interest throughout the civilized world. It seemed as if the day of wooden navies were over. Nor was it the superiority of iron as against wood that was settled by this combat ; it showed that a monitor was a better construction than a mailed broadside ship, and that inclined armor was inferior to a turret.

It may be interesting to know that the monitors proved to have serious defects as sea-going vessels. What became of the original Monitor? She foundered in a storm off Cape Hatteras during the same year. The Merrimac was blown up by the Confederates, when they abandoned Norfolk, in May, 1862.

IX

A THRILLING EXPERIENCE IN AN ARMY BALLOON

During General McClellan's campaign against Richmond, in 1862, balloons were often used to ascertain more accurately the position of the enemy's forces and fortifications.

The aeronaut of the Army of the Potomac was Professor Lowe. He had made seven thousand ascensions, and his army companion was usually either an artist, a correspondent, or a telegrapher.

A minute insulated wire reached from the car to headquarters, and McClellan was thus informed of all that could be seen within the Confederate works. Sometimes they remained aloft for hours, making observations with powerful glasses, and once or twice the enemy tested their distance with shell.

Heretofore the ascensions had been made from remote places, for there was good reason to believe that batteries lined the opposite hills ; but now, for the first time, Lowe intended to make an ascent whereby he could look into Richmond, count the forts encircling it,

and note the number and position of the camps that
intervened. The balloon was named the "Constitution," and looked like a semi-distended boa-constrictor,
as it flapped, with a jerking sound, and shook its oiled
and painted folds. It was anchored to the ground by
stout ropes tied to stakes, and also by sandbags which
were hooked to its netting. The basket lay alongside ;
the generators were contained in blue wooden wagons,
marked "U. S." ; and the gas was fed to the balloon
through rubber and metallic pipes. A tent or two, a
quantity of vitriol in green and wicker carboys, some
horses and transportation teams, and several men that
assisted the inflation, were the only objects to be remarked. As some time was to elapse before the
arrangements were completed, I went to one of the
tents to take a comfortable nap. The professor
aroused me at three o'clock, when I found the canvas
straining its bonds, and emitting a hollow sound, as of
escaping gas. The basket was made fast directly, the
telescopes tossed into place ; the professor climbed to
the side, holding by the network ; and I coiled myself
up in a rope at the bottom.

"Stand by your cables," he said, and the bags of
ballast were at once cut away. Twelve men took each
a rope in hand, and played out slowly, letting us glide

gently upward. The earth seemed to be falling away, and we poised motionless in the blue ether. The tree-tops sank downward, the hills dropped noiselessly through space, and directly the Chickahominy was visible beyond us, winding like a ribbon of silver through the ridgy landscape.

Far and wide stretched the Federal camps. We saw faces turned upward gazing at our ascent, and heard clearly, as in a vacuum, the voices of soldiers. At every second the prospect widened, the belt of horizon enlarged, remote farmhouses came in view; the earth was like a perfectly flat surface, painted with blue woods, and streaked with pictures of roads, fields, fences, and streams. As we rose higher, the river seemed directly beneath us, and the farms on the opposite bank were plainly discernible. Richmond lay only a little way off, enthroned on its many hills, with the James stretching white and sinuous from its feet to the horizon. We could see the streets, the suburbs, the bridges, the out-lying roads, nay, the moving masses of people. The Capitol sat, white and colossal, on Shockoe Hill, the dingy buildings of the Tredegar Works blackened the river-side above, and, one by one, we made out familiar hotels, public edifices, and vicinities. The fortifications were revealed in part only, for they took the hue of the soil, and blended with it ; but many camps were plainly discernible, and by means of the glasses we separated tent from tent and hut from hut. The Confederates were seen running to the cover of the woods, that we might not discover their numbers, but we knew the location of their campfires by the smoke that curled toward us.

A panorama so beautiful would have been rare at any time, but this was thrice interesting from its past and coming associations. Across those plains the hordes at our feet were either to advance victoriously, or be driven eastward with dusty banners and dripping hands. Those white farmhouses were to be receptacles for the groaning and the mangled ; thousands were to be received beneath the turf of those pasture fields ; and no rod of ground on any side that should not, sooner or later, smoke with the blood of the slain.

"Guess I've got 'em now, jest where I want 'em," said Lowe, with a gratified laugh ; "jest keep still as you mind to, and squint your eye through my glass, while I make a sketch of the roads and the country. Hold hard there, and anchor fast !" he screamed to the people below. Then he fell imperturbably to work, sweeping the country with his hawk-eye, and letting nothing escape that could contribute to the complete ness of his jotting.

We had been but a few minutes thus poised, when close below, from the edge of a timber stretch, puffed a volume of white smoke. A second afterward, the air quivered with the peal of a cannon. A third, and we heard the splitting shriek of a shell, that passed a little to our left, but in exact range, and burst beyond us in the ploughed field, heaving up the clay as it exploded.

"Ha!" said Lowe, "they have got us foul! Haul in the cables — quick!" he shouted in a fierce tone.

At the same instant, the puff, the report, and the shriek were repeated; but this time the shell burst to our right in mid-air, and scattered fragments around and below us.

"Another shot will do the business," said Lowe between his teeth; "it isn't a mile, and they have got the range."

Again the puff and the whizzing shock. I closed my eyes, and held my breath hard. The explosion was so close that the pieces of shell seemed driven across my face, and my ears quivered with the sound. I looked at Lowe to see if he was struck. He had sprung to his feet, and clutched the cordage frantically.

"Are you pulling in there, you men?" he bellowed with a loud imprecation.

"Puff! bang! whiz-z-z-z! splutter!" broke another shell, and my heart was wedged in my throat.

I saw at a glimpse the whole bright landscape again. I heard the voices of soldiers below, and saw them running across fields, fences, and ditches, to reach our anchorage. I saw some drummer boys digging in the field beneath for one of the buried shells. I saw the waving of signal flags, the commotion through the camps, — officers galloping their horses, teamsters whipping their mules, regiments turning out, drums beaten, and batteries limbered up. I remarked, last of all, the site of the battery that alarmed us, and, by a strange sharpness of sight and sense, believed that I saw the gunners swabbing, ramming, and aiming the pieces.

"Puff! bang! whiz-z-z-z! splutter! crash!"

"Puff! bang! whiz-z-z-z! splutter! crash!"

"My God!" said Lowe, hissing the words slowly and terribly, "they have opened upon us from another battery!"

The scene seemed to dissolve. A cold dew broke from my forehead. I grew blind and deaf. I had fainted.

"Throw some water in his face," said somebody.
"He ain't used to it. Hallo! there he comes to."

I staggered to my feet. There must have been a
thousand men about us. They were looking curiously
at the aeronaut and me. The balloon lay fuming and
struggling on the clods.

"Three cheers for the Union Bal-loon!" called a little fellow at my side.

"Hip, hip — hoorooar! hoorooar! hoorooar!"

"Tiger-r-r — yah! whoop!"

X

A PEN PICTURE OF ABRAHAM LINCOLN

THE most marked characteristic of President Lincoln's manners was his simplicity and artlessness.

This at once impressed itself upon the observation of those who met him for the first time, and each successive interview deepened the impression. People delighted to find in the ruler of the nation freedom from pomposity and affectation, mingled with a certain simple dignity which never forsook him, even in the presence of critical or polished strangers. There was always something which spoke the fine fibre of the man. While his disregard of courtly conventionalities was something ludi-

ABRAHAM LINCOLN.

crous, his native sweetness and straightforwardness of manner served to disarm criticism and impress the visitor that he was before a man, pure, self-poised, collected, and strong in unconscious strength.

The simple habits of Mr. Lincoln were so well known that it is a wonder that he did not sooner lose that precious life which he seemed to hold so lightly. He had an almost morbid dislike for an escort, or guard, and daily exposed himself to the deadly aim of an assassin. "If they kill me," he once said, "the next man will be just as bad for them; and in a country like this, where our habits are simple, and must be, assassination is always possible, and will come if they are determined upon it." A cavalry guard was once placed at the gates of the White House for a while, and he said, privately, that he "worried until he got rid of it."

Gentleness mixed with firmness characterized all of Mr. Lincoln's dealings with public men. Often bitterly assailed and abused, he never appeared to recognize the fact that he had political enemies. His keenest critics and most bitter opponents studiously avoided his presence. It seemed as if no man could be familiar with his homely, heart-lighted features, his single-hearted directness and manly kindliness, and remain long an enemy, or be anything but his friend. It was this warm frankness of Mr. Lincoln's manner that made a hard-headed politician once leave the hustings where Lincoln was speaking in 1856, saying, "I won't hear him, for I don't like a man that makes me believe in him in spite of myself."

"Honest old Abe" has passed into the language of our time and country as a synonym for all that is just and honest in man. Yet thousands of instances, unknown to the world, might be added to those already told of Lincoln's great and crowning virtue. This honesty appeared to spring from religious convictions. This was his surest refuge at times when he was most misunderstood or misrepresented. There was something touching in his childlike and simple reliance upon Divine aid, especially when in such extremities as he sometimes fell into. Though prayer and reading of the Scriptures were his constant habit, he more earnestly than ever, at such times, sought that strength which is promised when mortal help faileth. His address upon the occasion of his re-inauguration has been said to be as truly a religious document as a state-paper; and his acknowledgment of God and His providence are interwoven through all of his later speeches, letters, and messages. Once he said: "I have been. driven many times upon my knees by the overwhelming conviction that I had nowhere else to go. My own wisdom and that of all about me seemed insufficient for that day."

A certain lady lived for four years in the White House with President Lincoln's family. She gives the following incident of the sad days of 1863 : —

"One day, Mr. Lincoln came into the room where I was fitting a dress on Mrs. Lincoln. His step was slow and heavy, and his face sad. Like a tired child he threw himself upon a sofa, and shaded his eyes with his hands. He was a complete picture of dejection. Mrs. Lincoln, observing his troubled look, asked, —

"'Where have you been, father?'

"'To the War Department,' was the brief answer.

"'Any news?'

"'Yes, plenty of news, but no good news. It is dark, dark everywhere.'

"He reached forth one of his long arms and took a small Bible from a stand near the head of the sofa, opened the pages of the holy book, and was soon absorbed in reading them.

"A quarter of an hour passed, and, on glancing at the sofa, I saw that the face of the President seemed more cheerful. The dejected expression was gone, and the countenance seemed lighted up with new resolution and hope.

"The change was so marked that I could not but wonder at it, and wonder led to the desire to know what book of the Bible afforded so much comfort to the reader.

"Making the search for a missing article an excuse, I walked gently around the sofa, and, looking into the open book, I saw that Mr. Lincoln was reading that divine comforter, Job. He read with Christian eagerness, and the courage and hope that he derived from the inspired pages made him a new man.

"I almost imagined I could hear the Lord speaking to him from out the whirlwind of battle : 'Gird up now thy loins like a man; for I will demand of thee, and answer thou me.'

"What a sublime picture was this! The ruler of a mighty nation going to the pages of the Bible for comfort and courage — and finding both — in the darkest hours of his country's calamity."

No man but President Lincoln knew how great was the load of care which he bore, nor the amount of hard labor which he daily accomplished. With the usual perplexities of his great office, he carried the burdens of the Civil War, which he always called "this great trouble." Though the intellectual man had greatly grown, meantime, few people would recognize the hearty, blithe-

some, genial, and wiry Abraham Lincoln of earlier
days, with his stooping figure, dull eyes, careworn face,
and languid frame. The old, clear laugh never came
back; his even temper was sometimes disturbed, and
his natural charity for all was often turned into an
unwonted suspicion of the motives of men, whose selfish-
ness cost him so much wear of mind.

Lincoln did not have a hopeful temperament.
Although he tried to look at the bright side of things,
he was always prepared for disaster and defeat. He
often saw success when others saw disaster; but oftener
perceived a failure when others were elated with victory.
He was never weary of commending the patience of
the American people, which he thought something
matchless and touching. He would often shed tears
when speaking of the cheerful sacrifice of the light and
strength of so many homes throughout the land. His
own patience was marvellous. He was never crushed
at defeat or unduly elated by success. Once he said
the keenest blow of all the war was at an early stage,
when the disaster at Ball's Bluff, and the death of his
beloved friend, General Baker, smote upon him like a
whirlwind from a desert.

Mr. Lincoln loved to read the humorous writers. He
could repeat from memory whole chapters from the

chronicler of the "Mackerel Brigade," Parson Nasby, and "Private Miles O'Reilly." These light trifles diverted his mind, or, as he said, gave him refuge from himself and his weariness. The Bible was a very familiar study, whole chapters of Isaiah, the New Testament, and the Psalms, being fixed in his memory. He liked the Old Testament best, and dwelt on the simple beauty of the historical books. Of the poets, he preferred Tom Hood and Holmes, the mixture of humor and pathos in their writings being attractive to him beyond all other poets.

The President's love of music was something passionate, but his tastes were simple and uncultivated, his choice being old airs, songs, and ballads, among which the plaintive Scotch songs were best liked. "Annie Laurie," and especially "Auld Robin Gray," never lost their charms for him.

He wrote slowly and with greatest deliberation, and liked to take his time; yet some of his despatches, written without any corrections, were models of compactness and finish. His private correspondence was extensive. He preferred writing his letters with his own hand, making copies himself frequently, and filing everything away in a set of pigeon-holes in his office. He conscientiously attended to his enormous correspondence, and read everything that appeared to demand his attention. Even in the busiest days of the war, the good President found time to send his autograph to every schoolboy who wrote to him for it.

"None of the artists or pictures," says Walt Whitman, "caught the deep, though subtle and indirect expression of Lincoln's face. There is something else there. One of the great portrait painters of two or three centuries ago is needed.

"Probably the reader has seen physiognomies (often old farmers, sea-captains, and such) that, behind their homeliness, or even ugliness, held superior points so subtle, yet so palpable, making the real life of their faces almost as impossible to depict as a wild perfume, or fruit-paste, or a passionate tone of the living voice — and such was Lincoln's face, the peculiar color, the lines of it, the eyes, mouth, expression. Of technical beauty it had nothing — but to the eye of a great artist it furnished a rare study, a feast and fascination."

XI

HOW A BOY HELPED GENERAL M'CLELLAN WIN A BATTLE

Rich Mountain is famous as the scene where the first decisive battle was fought in West Virginia between General McClellan and the Confederate General Garnett. Rich Mountain Range is long, narrow, and high; and, except the summit, whereon is Mr. Hart's farm, it is covered with timber densely, save a narrow strip on one side, which is thickly covered with laurel. The Parkersburg and Staunton pike winds round the mountain, and passes, by the heads of ravines, directly over its top.

GEORGE B. M'CLELLAN.

The formation of the mountain-top is admirably adapted for the erection of strong military defences;

and on this account General Garnett had selected it as
a stronghold. He had erected formidable fortifications,
rendering an attack fatal to the assailing party, on the
road leading up the mountain, which was deemed the
only route by which the enemy could possibly reach his
position. General McClellan was advancing with an
army of five thousand men from Clarksburg, on the
turnpike, intending to attack Garnett early in the morning where his works crossed the road, not deeming any
other route up the mountain practicable. Had he carried his plan into execution, subsequent examination
showed that no earthly power could have saved him and
his army from certain defeat. The mountain was
steep in front of the fortifications; reconnoissance,
except in force, was impossible; and McClellan had
determined to risk a battle directly on the road, where
Garnett, without McClellan's knowledge, had rendered
his defences impervious to any power that man could
bring against him.

Mr. Hart, whose farm is on the mountain, was a
Union man, knew the ground occupied by Garnett, and
had carefully examined his fortifications on the road
coming up the mountain. Hearing that McClellan
was advancing, and fearing that he might attempt to
scale the works at the road, he sent his little son,

Joseph Hart, in the night, to meet McClellan and inform him of the situation of affairs on the mountain. Joseph, being but a boy, got through the Confederate lines without difficulty, and, travelling the rest of the night and part of the next day, reached the advanced guard of the Union army, informed them of the object of his coming, and was taken under guard to the general's quarters. Young as he was, the Federal commander looked upon him with suspicion. He questioned him closely. Joseph related in simple language all his father had told him of Garnett's position, the number of his force, the character of his works, and the impossibility of successfully attacking him on the mountain in the direction he proposed. The general listened attentively to his simple story, occasionally interrupting him with, " Tell the truth, my boy." At each interruption Joseph earnestly but quietly would reply, " I am telling you the truth, general." " But," says the latter, " do you know, if you are not, you will be shot as a spy?" " I am willing to be shot if all I say is not true," gently responded Joseph. " Well," says the general, after being satisfied of the entire honesty of his little visitor, "if I cannot go up the mountain by the road, in what way am I to go up?" Joseph, who now saw that he was believed from the manner of his interrogator, said there was a way up the other side, leaving the turnpike just at the foot, and going round the base to where the laurel was. There was no road there, and the mountain was very steep; but he had been up there; there were but few trees standing, and none fallen down to be in the way. The laurel was very thick up the side of the mountain, and the top matted together so closely that a man could walk on the tops. The last statement of Joseph once more awakened a slight suspicion of General McClellan, who said sharply, "Do you say men can walk on the tops of the laurel?" "Yes, sir," said Joseph. "Do you think my army can go up the mountain over the tops of the laurel?" "No, sir," promptly answered Joseph; "but *I* have done so, and a man might if he would walk slowly and have nothing to carry." "But, my boy, don't you see, I have a great many men, and horses, and cannon to take up, and how do you think we could get up over that laurel?" "The trees are small; they are so small you can cut them down, without making any noise, with knives and hatchets; and they will not know on the top of the mountain what you are doing or when you are coming," promptly and respectfully answered Joseph, who was now really to be the leader of the little army that was to decide the political destiny of West Virginia.

The Federal commander was satisfied with this ; and although he had marched all day, and intended that night to take the easy way up the mountain by the road, he immediately changed his plan of attack, and suddenly the army of the Union was moving away in the direction pointed out by Joseph Hart. When they came to the foot of the mountain, they left the smooth and easy track of the turnpike, and with difficulty wound round the broad base of the mountain through ravines and ugly gorges, to the point indicated by the little guide. Here the army halted. McClellan and some of his staff, with Joseph, proceeded to examine the nature of the ground, and the laurel covering the mountain from its base to its summit. All was precisely as Joseph had described it in the general's tent on the Staunton pike ; and the quick eye of the hero of Rich Mountain saw at a glance the feasibility of the attack. It was past midnight when the army reached the foot of the mountain. Though floating clouds hid the stars, the night was not entirely dark, and more than a thousand knives and hatchets were soon busy clearing away the marvellous laurel. Silence reigned throughout the lines, save the sharp click of the small blades and the rustle of the falling laurel. Before daybreak the narrow and precipitous way was cleared, and the work of

ascending commenced. The horses were tied at the
foot of the mountain. The artillery horses were taken
from the carriages. One by one the cannon were taken
up the rough and steep side of the mountain by hand,
and left within a short distance of the top, in such a
situation as to be readily moved forward when the moment of attack should arrive. The main army then
commenced the march up by companies, many falling
down, but suddenly recovering their places. The ascent
was a slow and tedious one. The way was winding and
a full mile. But before daybreak all was ready, and the
Union cannon were booming upon and over the enemy's
works, nearly in the rear, at an unexpected moment, and
from an entirely unexpected quarter. They were thun-
der-struck, as well as struck by shell and canister.
They did the best they could by a feeble resistance, and
fled precipitately down the mountain, pursued by the
Federals to Cheat River, where the brave Garnett was
killed. Two hundred brave men fell on the mountain,
and were buried by the side of the turnpike, with no
other sign of the field of interment than a long indenta-
tion made by the sinking down of the earth in the line
where the bodies lay at rest.

XII

OLD ABE, THE SOLDIER BIRD

ONE day, in the spring of 1861, Chief Sky, a Chippewa Indian, living in the northern wilds of Wisconsin, captured an eagle's nest. To make sure of his prize, he cut the tree down, and caught the eaglets as they were sliding from the nest to run and hide in the grass. One died. He took the other home and built it a nest in a tree close by his wigwam. The eaglet was as big as a hen, covered with soft brown down. The red children were delighted with their new pet; and as soon as it got acquainted it liked to sit down in the grass and see them play with the dogs. But Chief Sky was poor, and he had to sell it to a white man for a bushel of corn. The white man brought it to Eau Claire, a little village alive with men going to the war. "Here's a recruit," said the man. "An eagle, an eagle!" shouted the soldiers, "let him enlist;" and, sure enough, he was sworn into the service with ribbons, red, white, and blue, round his neck.

On a perch surmounted by stars and stripes, the

company took him to Madison, the capital of the State. As they marched into camp, with colors flying, drums beating, and the people cheering, the eagle seized the flag in his beak and spread his wings, his bright eye kindling with the spirit of the scene. Shouts rent the air : "The bird of Columbia ! the eagle of freedom forever !" The State made him a new perch, the boys named him "Old Abe," and the regiment, the Eighth Wisconsin, was henceforth called "the Eagle regiment." On the march it was carried at the head of the company, and everywhere was greeted with delight. At St. Louis, a gentleman offered five hundred dollars for it, and another his farm. No, no, the boys had no notion to part with their bird. It was above all price, an emblem of battle and of victory. Besides, it interested their minds, and made them think less of hardships and of home.

I cannot tell you all the droll adventures of the bird through its three years of service, its flights in the air, its fights with the guinea-hens, and its race with the darkies. When the regiment was in summer quarters it was allowed to run at large, and every morning went to the river half a mile off, where it splashed and played in the water to its heart's content, faithfully returning to camp when it had enough. Old Abe's

favorite place of resort was the sutler's tent, where a
live chicken found no quarter in his presence. But
rations got low, and for two days Abe had nothing to
eat. Hard-tack he objected to, fasting was disagreeable, and Tom, his bearer, could not get beyond the
pickets to a farmyard. At last, pushing his way to the
colonel's tent, he pleaded for poor Abe. The colonel
gave him a pass, and Tom got him an excellent dinner.

One day a farmer asked Tom to come and show the
eagle to his children. Satisfying the curiosity of the
family, Tom set him down in the barnyard. Oh, what
a screeching and scattering among the fowls; for what
should Abe do but pounce upon one and gobble up
another, to the great disgust of the farmer, who declared that was not the bargain. Abe thought, however, there was no harm in confiscating, nor did Tom.

He seemed to have sense enough to know that he was
a burden to his bearer on the march. He would occasionally spread his wings and soar aloft to a great height,
the men all along the line of march cheering him as he
went up. He regularly received his rations from the
commissary, the same as any enlisted man. Whenever
fresh meat was scarce he would go on a foraging expedition himself. He would be gone two or three days, but
would always return, and generally with a young lamb

or a chicken in his talons. However far he might fly in search of food, he was always sure to find his regiment again. In what way he distinguished the two armies so accurately that he was never known to mistake the gray for the blue, no one can tell. But so it was, that he was never known to alight save in his own regiment, and amongst his own men.

Abe was in twenty battles, besides many skirmishes. He was at the siege of Vicksburg, the storming of Corinth, and marched with Sherman up the Red River. The whiz of bullets and the scream of shell were his delight. As the battle grew hot and hotter, he would flap his wings and mingle his wildest notes with the noise around him. He was very fond of music, especially " Yankee Doodle " and " Old John Brown." Upon parade, he always gave heed to " Attention." With his eye on the commander, he would listen and obey orders, noting time accurately. After parade he would put off his soldierly air, flap his wings, and make himself at home. The Confederates called him " Yankee Buzzard," " Owl, Owl," and other hard names ; but his eagle nature was quite above noticing it.

The Confederate General Price gave orders to his men to be sure and capture the eagle of the Eighth Wisconsin. He would rather have it than a dozen battle-flags. But for all that he scarcely lost a feather, only one from his right wing. His tail feathers were once cropped by a bullet.

The shield on which he was carried, however, showed so many marks of the enemy's bullets, that it looked on the top as if a groove plane had been run over it.

At last the war came to an end, and the brave Wisconsin Eighth, with its live eagle and torn and riddled flags, was welcomed back to Madison. It went out a thousand strong, and returned a little band, scarred and toil-worn, having fought and won.

And what of the soldier bird? In the name of his gallant veterans he was presented to the State. The Governor accepted the illustrious gift, and ample quarters were provided for him in the beautiful State House grounds.

Nor was the end yet. At the great fair in Chicago, an enterprising gentleman invited "Abe" to attend. He had colored photographs of the old hero struck off, and sold many thousands of dollars' worth for the benefit of poor and sick soldiers.

At the centennial celebration, held in Philadelphia in 1876, "Old Abe" occupied a prominent place on his perch on the west side of the nave in the Agricultural Building. He was still alive, though evidently growing old, and was the observed of all the observers. Thousands of visitors, from all sections of the country, paid their respects to the grand old bird.

The soldier who had carried him during the war continued to have charge of him after the war was over, until the day of Old Abe's death, which occurred in 1881.

XIII

A BOY'S EXPERIENCE AT THE BATTLE OF FREDERICKSBURG

[*From the "Youth's Companion."*]

I WAS but seventeen years of age when I enlisted in a Maine regiment. We were not brought face to face with the enemy until December, 1862, when the great battle of Fredericksburg was fought. The morning of December 11 found us opposite Fredericksburg, which is situated on the south side of the Rappahannock River. We spent the entire day in watching our batteries throwing shells over into the burning city. With the aid of a glass we could see the enemy's works, stretching far down the river. That night their camp-fires were plainly visible, and at times faint cheers were wafted to us on the evening breeze.

The engineer corps was endeavoring to lay pontoon bridges for our army to cross upon. The Confederate sharp-shooters hotly contested the laying of the bridges, and many a poor fellow lost his life that day. But at last they were ready for us, and on the morning of the

CROSSING THE RAPPAHANNOCK ON A PONTOON.

12th, in a dense fog, we crossed over, about two miles below the city. Our supply of food was rather limited, and, warned by past experiences, I dined and supped on parched corn and hot coffee. I slept soundly upon the frozen ground that night, and long before daybreak the next morning the whole army was astir, and we had cooked and eaten a hasty breakfast.

The Rappahannock River, upon whose banks we lay, runs in a south-easterly direction. Back a distance of about a mile rise the heights of Fredericksburg, at the foot of which runs the railroad to Richmond; and behind the railroad embankment and upon the heights were intrenched the Confederates. About half-way between the heights and the river, and running nearly parallel with the latter, is the Bowling Green turnpike. The right of our line of battle extended above the city, but we were on the left.

At sunrise our brigade began to move toward the turnpike. We had scarcely marched a dozen yards before the Confederates opened fire on us. I could not refrain from laughing aloud when I saw how nimbly the captain of my company, who had been under fire before, dodged the shells as they came over our heads, but I soon learned to do it myself, and then thought it no joke. We double-quicked to the turnpike, where we found shelter by lying flat upon our faces in a ditch, while the shells went bursting over us with such frightful noises that I hugged the earth for life. I know of no sound so horrible as the fiendish music which comes from the flying pieces of a burst shell.

Our batteries replied to the fire with promptness and energy ; and the sharp and almost continuous rattle of musketry told us that the battle was in progress. Aids and mounted orderlies went dashing hither and thither in hot haste, bearing orders to the various commands, and generals with their staffs were gathered in groups anxiously scanning the Confederate movements through field-glasses. Great clouds of smoke settled over us, like that from a burning city, and half obscured the columns of men who were marching with quick step, and "swiftly forming in the ranks of war." Bugles blared and drums beat, and a little to my right and front, high above the din of battle, rose the shrill cry of some poor, wounded soul.

The first one killed in our regiment was a noble young fellow from my company, who was struck in the back by a spent cannon-ball. We had time to dig him a shallow grave with our bayonets before we moved forward.

A little after noon, word was given to prepare for the

advance. Between us and the Confederates, a distance
of nearly half a mile, lay an open, level field, where
corn had been planted the preceding summer. The
ground, frozen the night before, and thawed again at
midday, was miry and treacherous, and we often sank
half-way to our knees. At intervals deep ditches had
once been dug for drainage.

General R——, commanding our brigade, rode down
the line and gave us words of encouragement.

"Boys," said he, "don't dodge when"—but before
he could finish the sentence a shell whizzed so close to
his head that he himself dodged very emphatically.

With a laugh he added, "But you *may* dodge when
they come as close as that!"

Then we gave three cheers for our general, who, if
he did dodge, was a brave and kind man.

Now our line moved forward a dozen yards.

"Halt! Unsling knapsacks! Fix bayonets!"

Then I knew we were to fight the Confederates with
cold steel.

Down the line came the order again, "Forward!"
The bullets now began to sing angrily about our ears,
and our men began to fall. The one with whom I
touched elbows on my left was among the first victims.
The ball entered his leg with a sickening "thud,"

and he fell to the ground with a cry of "Oh, I'm shot!"

The company to which I belonged was the "color company," and the two brave fellows who carried the flags, as soon as the order to move forward was given, stepped out of the ranks in advance of the others, and maintained that position during the charge. It was a daring deed, for the sharp-shooters always seek to pick off the color-bearers.

Down to this time I had felt nervous; my knees trembled, and my legs were weak. I confess that I was afraid; but being afraid, and yielding to fear, are two different things. When my mother bade me good-by, the day my regiment left for Washington, she said, " I shall expect always to hear that you have done your duty." The remembrance of her pale face was, of itself, enough to make one brave. But I needed no such incentive; when I saw my comrades falling on every side, fear left me, and, young as I was, my anger was roused, and I believe I could have fought a whole army.

Now came the order, "Charge bayonets! Forward, double-quick!" We had a quarter of a mile of muddy ground to cross, and deep ditches to leap down into and clamber out of in the midst of a terrible fire. With

each advancing step, the fire of the Confederates increased, and the air was filled with bursting shells, grape
and canister and rifle balls. So thickly did this deadly
hail fall around us that the mud and dirt were con
stantly spattering in my face. Instinctively we bowed
our heads to this fierce storm as we swept on.

There were great gaps in our ranks, as our company,
one after another, fell under the awful fire; but there
was no flinching, no hesitation, as with swift steps and
stern faces we swept across the few remaining yards of
ground between us and that long row of levelled rifles
from which were belching forth death and destruction.
With a wild, determined cry our regiment leaped upon
them. There was only a brief struggle, when the Confederates fell back up the heights, followed a short distance by our troops.

But I never reached the intrenchment myself. When
we were almost upon it, and I was grasping my rifle
firmly, expecting in a moment to use it, I found myself
flat upon the ground, and heard the captain, as the company passed over my body, shout, "Lay low, boy!"
Then I realized that I had been hit. For a few moments I lay perfectly still; then I determined to make
a desperate effort to get off the field, for I feared our
men might be driven back again.

I dared not examine my wound lest I should faint, and so fall into the hands of the Confederates. Finding that I could make some progress by using my rifle as a support, I slowly and painfully dragged myself to the rear. The battle was still raging behind me with un-abated force, and the shot and shells from our own, as well as the Confederate batteries, were passing over my head with a deafening noise. On every side lay the dead and wounded, and the groans and appeals for help were pitiful to hear.

At last I reached the turnpike, and beneath its shelter I first examined the nature of my injury. I was overjoyed to find that the supposed wound was only a very severe bruise. An army cup which I carried on the outside, and a tin plate and my stock of hard bread which were inside my knapsack, had saved me. The force of the bullet was such that it had taken a piece clear out of the cup, which was made of thick material; and it passed through the plate and the hard bread, and did not fairly enter my flesh. I still have the piece which was torn from my cup.

I was sent to the hospital for a few days, until I could march again.

As I had surmised, the survivors of our regiment were finally driven back from the position they had, at so fearful a cost, won. When the sixty rounds of ammunition which were in their cartridge-boxes had been fired away, and no fresh cartridges were sent, there was nothing left for them to do but to fall back.

From the time our regiment left the turnpike, on the charge, until it returned, was, I think, hardly an hour. We started on with less than five hundred men, and in that brief time we lost, in killed, wounded, and missing, over two hundred and fifty, more than one-half. My own company lost thirty-three out of fifty.

Some years ago I revisited the battle-field. The bodies of the fallen had been gathered into the soldiers' cemetery just back of the city, and near the deadly stone wall where the right of our army was engaged. I walked down the turnpike to where we fought. Nature had obliterated nearly every sign of the conflict, and the miry field across which we charged on that eventful December day was covered with waving corn. The sun shone as clearly, the birds sang as sweetly, and the flowers bloomed as brightly, as if that field had never been ploughed with shot and shell, and fertilized with the blood of brave men.

XIV

THE STORY OF SHERIDAN'S FAMOUS RIDE

The stirring lines of Buchanan Read's well-known poem called "Sheridan's Ride" are familiar as household

PHILIP H. SHERIDAN.

words to the boys and girls of our day. This poem has been read and recited for many years by American school children. It has always been a favorite, for it records in verse the gallant deed of one of the most brilliant and successful generals in the war for the Union.

The victory gained by General Sheridan at Cedar Creek, Va., October 19, 1864, surpassed in interest the victory gained precisely one month earlier at Winchester. It was a victory following upon the heels of apparent reverse, and therefore reflecting peculiar

SHERIDAN'S CAVALRY MAKING A CHARGE.

credit on the brave commander to whose timely
arrival upon the field the final success of the day must
be attributed.

The general was at Winchester in the early morning
when the enemy attacked — twenty miles distant from
the field of operations. General Wright was in command. The enemy had approached under cover of a
heavy fog, and, flanking the extreme right of the
Federal line, held by General Crook's corps, and attacking in the centre, had thrown the entire line into
confusion, and driven it several miles. The enemy
was pushing on, turning against the Union forces a
score of guns already captured from them.

Sheridan's victorious and hitherto invincible army was
routed and in disorderly retreat before a confident enemy.
The roads were crowded with wagons and ambulances
hurrying to the rear, while the fields were alive with
wounded, stragglers, and disorganized troops without officers, without arms, and without courage — all bent on
being the first to carry the news of the disaster back to
Winchester.

> " Up from the south, at break of day,
> Bringing to Winchester fresh dismay,
> The affrighted air with a shudder bore,
> Like a herald in haste, to the chieftain's door,
> The terrible grumble and rumble and roar,
> Telling the battle was on once more,
> And Sheridan twenty miles away."

A brave nucleus of the army, which had not shared
in the surprise and subsequent demoralization, was
fighting with determined pluck to prevent disaster from
becoming disgrace. The universal thought, and, in
varying phrase, the spontaneous utterance, was : "Oh,
for one hour of Sheridan !"   But Sheridan was twenty
miles away, at Winchester, where he had arrived the
day before from Washington.

At this juncture, those who were stationed near the
Winchester pike heard, far to the rear, a faint cheer go
up, as a hurrying horseman passed a group of wounded
soldiers, and dashed down that historic road toward the
line of battle.   As he drew nearer, it was seen that the
coal-black horse was flecked with foam, both horse and
rider grimed with dust, and the dilated nostrils and
laboring breath of the former told of a race both long
and swift.

> " But there is a road to Winchester town,
>   A good, broad highway, leading down ;
> · And there, through the flush of the morning light,
>   A steed, as black as the steeds of night,
>   Was seen to pass as with eagle flight :
>   As if he knew the terrible need,
>   He stretched away with his utmost speed."

A moment more, and a deafening cheer broke from
the troops in that part of the field, as they recognized

in the coming horseman the looked-for Sheridan. Above the roar of musketry and artillery, that shout arose like a cry of victory. The news flashed from brigade to brigade along the front with telegraphic speed ; and then, as Sheridan, cap in hand, dashed along the rear of the straggling line, thus confirming to all eyes the fact of his arrival, a continuous cheer burst from the whole army. Hope took the place of fear, courage the place of despondency, cheerfulness the place of gloom. The entire aspect of things seemed changed in a moment. Further retreat was no longer thought of. Order came out of chaos, an army out of a rabble.

Sheridan's leadership perfectly restored the courage and spirit of the army. It had got over its panic, and was again ready for business. Generals rode out to meet him, officers waved their swords, and men threw up their caps.

General Custer, discovering Sheridan at the moment he arrived, rode up to him, threw his arms around his neck, and kissed him on the cheek. Waiting for no other parley than simply to exchange greeting, and to say, " This retreat must be stopped ! " Sheridan broke loose and began galloping down the lines, along the whole front of the army. Everywhere the enthusiasm caused by his appearance was the same.

" And the wave of retreat checked its course there, because
The sight of the master compelled it to pause.
With foam and with dust the black charger was gray.
By the flash of his eye, and his red nostrils' play,
He seemed to the whole great army to say:
' I have brought you Sheridan, all the way
From Winchester down, to save you the day!'"

The line was speedily reformed; provost-marshals
brought in stragglers by the scores; the retreating
army turned its face to the foe. An attack just about
to be made by the latter was repulsed, and the tide of
battle turned. Then Sheridan's time was come. A
cavalry charge was ordered against right and left flank
of the enemy, and then a grand advance of the three
infantry corps from left to right on the enemy's centre.
On through Middletown, and beyond, the Confederates
hurried, and the Army of the Shenandoah pursued.
The roar of musketry now had a gleeful, dancing sound.
The guns fired shotted salutes of victory. Custer and
Merritt, charging in on right and left, doubled up the
flanks of the foe, taking prisoners, slashing, killing,
driving as they went. The march of the infantry was
more majestic and terrible. The lines of the foe
swayed and broke before it everywhere. Beyond
Middletown, on the battle-field fought over in the morning, their columns were completely overthrown and dis-

organized. They fled along the pike and over the fields like sheep.

Thus on through Strasburg with two brigades of cavalry at their heels. Two thousand prisoners were gathered together, though there was not a sufficient guard to send them all to the rear. The guns lost in the morning were recaptured, and as many more taken, making fifty in all, and, according to Sheridan's report, the enemy reached Mount Jackson without an organized regiment. The scene at Sheridan's headquarters at night after the battle was wildly exciting. General Custer arrived about nine o'clock. The first thing he did was to hug General Sheridan with all his might, lifting him in the air, and whirling him around and around, with the shout: "God be praised, we've cleaned them out and got the guns!" Catching sight of General Torbert, Custer went through the same proceeding with him, until Torbert was forced to cry out: "There, there, old fellow, don't capture me!"

Sheridan's ride to the front, October 19, 1864, will go down in history as one of the most important and thrilling events which have ever given interest to a battle scene. Stripped of all poetic gloss, and analyzed after more than a quarter of a century of peace, the result achieved by Sheridan's matchless generalship, after he reached his shattered army on the field of Cedar Creek, as an illustration of the wonderful influence of one man over many, and as an example of snatching a great victory from an appalling defeat, still stands without a parallel in history.

> " Hurrah, hurrah, for Sheridan !
> Hurrah, hurrah, for horse and man !
> And when their statues are placed on high,
> Under the dome of the Union sky —
> The American soldier's Temple of Fame —
> There with the glorious general's name,
> Be it said, in letters both bold and bright :
> ' Here is the steed that saved the day
> By carrying Sheridan into the fight,
> From Winchester twenty miles away ! ' "

XV

THE CAVALRY CHARGE

WITH bray of the trumpet
And roll of the drum,
And keen ring of bugles,
The cavalry come.
Sharp clank the steel scabbards,
The bridle-chains ring,
And foam from red nostrils
The wild chargers fling.

Tramp! tramp! o'er the green sward
That quivers below,
Scarce held by the curb-bit,
The fierce horses go!
And the grim-visaged colonel,
With ear-rending shout,
Peals forth to the squadrons
The order, "Trot out!"

One hand on the sabre,
    And one on the rein,
The troopers move forward
    In line on the plain.
As rings the word "Gallop!"
    The steel scabbards clank,
And each rowel is pressed
    To a horse's hot flank;
And swift is their rush
    As the wild torrent's flow,
When it pours from the crag
    On the valley below.

"Charge!" thunders the leader.
    Like shaft from the bow
Each mad horse is hurled
    On the wavering foe.
A thousand bright sabres
    Are gleaming in air;
A thousand dark horses
    Are dashed on the square.

Resistless and reckless
    Of aught may betide,
Like demons, not mortals,
    The wild troopers ride.

Cut right ! and cut left !
　For the parry who needs ?
The bayonets shiver
　Like wind-shattered reeds !

Vain — vain the red volley
　That bursts from the square —
The random-shot bullets
　Are wasted in air.
Triumphant, remorseless,
　Unerring as death, —
No sabre that's stainless
　Returns to its sheath.

The wounds that are dealt
　By that murderous steel
Will never yield case
　For the surgeons to heal.
Hurrah ! they are broken —
　Hurrah ! boys, they fly —
None linger save those
　Who but linger to die.

Rein up your hot horses,
　And call in your men ;
The trumpet sounds " Rally
　To color " again.

Some saddles are empty,
  Some comrades are slain,
And some noble horses
  Lie stark on the plain ;
But war's a chance game, boys,
  And weeping is vain.

XVI

THE DESTRUCTION OF THE ALBEMARLE

ONE of the most daring and successful exploits of
the late war was performed by a brave and intrepid
young naval officer. To Lieutenant William B. Cushing was due the destruction of the famous Confederate
ram called the Albemarle. This powerful ironclad had
become a formidable obstruction to the occupation of
the North Carolina sounds by the Union forces.

During the summer of 1864, Lieutenant Cushing,
commanding the Monticello, one of the sixteen vessels
engaged in watching the ram, conceived the plan of
destroying their antagonist by means of a torpedo.
Upon submitting the plan to Rear-Admiral Lee and the
Navy Department, he was detached from his vessel,
and sent to New York to provide the articles necessary
for his purpose, and, these preparations having been at
last completed, he returned again to the scene of action.
His plan was to affix his newly contrived torpedo appa-
ratus to one of the picket launches — little steamers
not larger than a seventy-four's launch, but fitted with

a compact engine, and designed to relieve the seamen of the fatigue of pulling about at night on the naval picket line — and of which half a dozen had been then recently built.   Under Lieutenant Cushing's supervision, picket launch No. 1 was supplied with the torpedo, which was carried in a basket, fixed to a long arm, which could be propelled, at the important moment, from the vessel, in such a manner as to reach the side of the vessel to be destroyed, there to be fastened, and exploded at the will of those in the torpedo boat, without serious risk to themselves.   Having prepared his boat, he selected thirteen men, six of whom were officers, to assist him in the undertaking.   His first attempt to reach the Albemarle failed, as his boat got aground and was only with difficulty released.   On the following night, however, he again set out upon his perilous duty, determined and destined this time to succeed.   Moving cautiously, with muffled oars, up the narrow Roanoke, he skilfully eluded the observation of the numerous forts and pickets with which that river was lined, and, passing within twenty yards of a picket vessel, without detection, he soon found himself abreast of the town of Plymouth.   The night was very dark and stormy, and, having thus cleared the pickets, the launch crossed to the other side of the river, opposite

the town, and, sweeping round, came down upon the
Albemarle from up the stream. The ram was moored
near a wharf, and, by the light of a large campfire on
the shore, Cushing saw a large force of infantry, and
also discerned that the ironclad was protected by a
boom of pine logs which extended about twenty feet
from her. The watch on the Albemarle knew nothing
of his approach till he was close upon them, when they
hailed, "What boat is that?" and were answered,
"The Albemarle's boat;" and the same instant the
launch struck, "bows on," against the boom of logs,
crushing them in about ten feet, and running its bows
upon them. She was immediately greeted with a heavy
and incessant infantry fire from the shore, while the
ports of the Albemarle were opened, and a gun trained
upon the daring party. Cushing promptly replied with
a dose of canister, but the gallant young fellow had
enough for one man to manage. He had a line attached to his engineer's leg, to pull in lieu of bell
signals; another line to detach the torpedo, and
another to explode it; besides this, he managed the
boom which was to place the torpedo under the vessel,
and fired the howitzer with his own hand. But he
coolly placed the torpedo in its place and exploded it.
At the same moment he was struck on the right wrist

with a musket ball, and a shell from the Albemarle went crashing through the launch. The whole affair was but the work of a few minutes. Each man had now to save himself as best he might. Cushing threw off his coat and shoes, and, leaping into the water, struck out for the opposite shore ; but, the cries of one of his drowning men attracting the enemy's fire, he turned down the stream. The water was exceedingly cold, and his heavy clothing rendered it very difficult for him to keep afloat ; and after about an hour's swimming he went ashore, and fell exhausted upon the bank. On coming to his senses, he found himself near a sentry and two officers, who were discussing the affair, and heard them say that Cushing was dead. Thinking that he had better increase the distance between the rebels and himself, he managed to shove himself along on his back, by working with his heels against the ground, until he reached a place of concealment.

After dark, he proceeded through the swamp for some distance, lacerating his feet and hands with the briers and oyster shells. He next day met an old negro whom he thought he could trust. The negro was frightened at Cushing's wild appearance, and tremblingly asked who he was. "I am a Yankee," replied Cushing, "and I am one of the men who blew up the Albemarle."

DESTRUCTION OF THE ALBEMARLE.

"My golly, massa!" said the negro, "dey kill you if
dey catch you ; you dead gone sure!" Cushing asked
him if he could trust him to go into the town and bring
him back the news. The negro assented, and Cushing
gave him all the money he had and sent him off. He
then climbed up a tree and opened his jack-knife, the
only weapon he had, and prepared for any attack which
might be made.

After a time the negro came back, and, to Cushing's
joy, reported the Albemarle sunk and the people leaving the town. Cushing then went farther down the
river, and found a boat on the opposite bank belonging
to a picket guard. He once more plunged into the
chilly river and detached the boat, but, not daring to
get into it, left it drift down the river, keeping himself
concealed. At last, thinking he was far enough away
to elude observation, he got into the boat and paddled
for eight hours until he reached the squadron. After
hailing them, he fell into the bottom of the boat, utterly
exhausted by hunger, cold, fatigue, and excitement, to
the surprise of the people in the squadron, who were
somewhat distrustful of him when he first hailed, thinking him a rebel who was trying some trick.

Nothing, indeed, but an overruling Providence and an
iron will ever saved Cushing from death. He saw two

of his men drown, who were stronger than he, and said
of himself that when he paddled his little boat his arms
and his will were the only living parts of his organization.

One man of the party returned, having been picked
up after he had travelled across the country and been
in the swamps nearly two days.

But one or two were wounded, and the larger part
were captured by the rebels, being unable to extricate
themselves from their perilous position among the logs
of the boom, under the guns of the ram. The Albemarle had one of her bows stove in by the explosion of
the torpedo, and sank at her moorings within a few moments, without loss of life to her crew. Her fate
opened the river to the Union forces, who quickly occupied Plymouth; the North Carolina sounds were again
cleared from rebel craft, and the large fleet of vessels
which had been occupied in watching the ironclad were
released from that arduous duty.

Lieutenant Cushing, to whose intrepidity and skill
the country was indebted for this and many other dashing exploits, was engaged in thirty-five naval combats
during the war. What a glorious record for a young
man twenty-three years old! He died at the age of
thirty-two, the youngest officer of his rank in the United
States Navy.

.

.

XVII

THE FINAL STRUGGLE AT GETTYSBURG

[*From Henry Ward Beecher's "Norwood."*]

On the third day of July, 1863, and the third of the complex battle of Gettysburg, General Lee, having in vain assaulted the left of the Union line on the day before, determined to break through the centre, and at the same time to enlarge the hold which he had secured upon the extreme Union right, on the eastern slope of Culp's Hill. But by four in the morning General Meade attacked the intrusive forces which had thus, while yesterday's battle raged on the extreme left, as it were, stolen in on the right, and by eleven o'clock they were driven out, thus anticipating and defeating Lee's intention of turning the Union right.

A wonderful 'silence now came over the vast battle-field and brooded for the space of two hours. Birds sang again, though the ground beneath them was covered with unburied men. The rustling of leaves could be heard once more by the men who lay resting under the trees. But the very silence, that usually brings all thoughts of peace, now sharpened men's fears. It was like that dreadful calm which precedes the burst of storms. Just such it was. At one o'clock it was broken by an uproar as wonderful as had been the silence. Two hundred and thirty-five cannon joined in a clangor of death, such as had never been heard upon this continent. Lee had concentrated a hundred and forty-five guns over against the centre of Cemetery Ridge, and Meade replied with eighty guns — all that could be well placed in his narrower space. The other battle before seemed noiseless compared with this immense cannonading. The slopes of Oak Ridge and the swells upon the further side of the valley seemed on fire. Each little hill-top became a volcano. From the right, from the left, from the centre, battery upon battery, and parks of batteries flamed and thundered. The smoke rolled up white and bluish gray, as storm-clouds lift and roll up the sides of mountains. From every direction came the flying missiles — cross-ploughing Cemetery Hill with hideous furrows, in which to plant dead men. Shot flew clear over the ridge — caissons sheltered behind the hill were reached and blown up. Horses standing harnessed to reserved artillery, in places before secure, were smitten down. Strange was the discordant music of the missile sounds, for which

there were no pauses, that filled the air. Some went
hissing, some flew with muffled growl, some shook out
a gushing sound like the rush of waters; some carried
with them an intense and malignant howl; some spit
and sputtered in a spiteful manner; others whirred or
whistled, or spun threads of tenor or treble sounds.
But, whatever the variety in this awful aërial music, all
meant death. If a thousand meteors had burst, and
each one flung down shattered masses of meteoric stone,
it would have scarcely seemed more like a deluge of
iron rain than now it did. Orderlies and aids found the
roads and fields on the far side of the hill, safe before,
now raining with bullets. Meade's headquarters were
riddled, and his staff driven to another quarter. In
half an hour all the fields were cleared and the men
were under cover. Fortunately, the enemy's artillery
was elevated too much. The Union soldiers escaped
with comparatively little harm, while the reverse of the
hill was excoriated with shot and shell. In the burial-
ground on the head of Cemetery Ridge, projecting
toward the village of Gettysburg, fell the iron hail,
rending the graves and splintering the monuments.
Flowers growing on graves were rudely picked by
hurtling iron. Soldiers who had fallen at Fair Oaks,
and had been brought here for burial, far away from all

thought of battle, in this quiet Pennsylvania vale, were still pursued by war, which rudely tore up their graves; and they heard again the thunder of battle swelling above these resting-places, where, it would seem, they should have found quiet.

When it had thundered and rained iron for more than two hours, there came moving across the valley fifteen thousand men to take possession of that ridge! As they moved from afar the Union artillery smote them; but they did not heed it. As they drew near, still rent by shot and shell, — earnest, eager, brave, — there burst upon their right flank a fire of musketry and artillery that quite crumpled up and swung back their men upon their centre. Next, their left wing was utterly riddled and routed by the sharpness of the musketry; and what part was not captured fled and escaped. But the massive centre, with men as brave as ever faced death, stern, headlong, pushed right up to General Hancock's lines, and across them, but could come no further! Like a ship whose impetus carried it far up upon a shoal, from which it cannot recede when it would, several brigades had shot, by the terrible momentum, so far up that when from the slopes of the cemetery, and from the artillery on Meade's left wing, they were enfiladed, while Hancock, with fresh brigades drawn from his left, met them in front with a fire that pierced like a flame, they yielded themselves up. They had gotten the hill for which they came, but not as victors. The rest shrunk, driven backward, sharply raked with artillery and scorched with sheets of musketry, got them out of the battle, and fled across the valley to their lines, whence they should come no more out hitherward. Many that longed to go with them lay with pitiful wounds. A thousand that an hour before were fierce in ambitious expectation, now and never more cared what befell them, nor what happened under the sun! When the sun went down on that 3d of July, the Union army, a mighty sufferer in more than twenty thousand slain and wounded men, yet had never such cause of rejoicing for the coming anniversary day as now, when all those thousands of men joyfully had died or suffered wounds to preserve that nation's life whose birthday is celebrated on the Fourth of July!

The morning of Saturday, the Fourth of July, rose fair over Gettysburg. Ewell's corps of Lee's army withdrew from the town, and Howard's troops immediately took possession.

There was great joy throughout the Union army. Officers congratulated each other ; the men were raised to the proudest exultation. The Army of the Potomac, the victim of misfortunes, but always a model of indomitable patience, had at length met their great antagonist in a long and severe fight, and thoroughly defeated him.   While all were exhilarated with the immediate victory, the thoughtful men of the army experienced a deeper gladness in their prescience of the scope of this victory in its relation to public affairs.   The climax was reached.   Henceforward the Confederate cause was subject to decline, weakness, and extinction.

XVIII

LINCOLN'S GETTYSBURG SPEECH

WHEN Abraham Lincoln had gained the people's ear, men noticed that he scarcely made a speech or wrote a state paper in which there was not an illustration or a quotation from the Bible. He had been thoroughly instructed in it by his mother. It was the one book always found in the pioneer's cabin, and to which she, being a woman of deep religious feeling, turned for sympathy and guidance. Out of it she taught her boy to spell and read, and with its poetry, histories, and principles she so familiarized him that they always influenced his subsequent life.

In the good President's religious faith two leading ideas were prominent from first to last — man's helplessness, both as to strength and wisdom, and God's helpfulness in both.

To a friend who anxiously asked him in the dark days of 1862: "Do you think we shall succeed?" he said, "I believe our cause is just; I believe that we shall conquer in the end. I should be very glad to take

my neck out of the yoke and go back to my old home
and my old life at Springfield. But it has pleased
Almighty God to place me in this position ; and, looking
up to Him for support, I must discharge my destiny as
best I can."

The words of Lincoln seemed to grow more clear and
more remarkable as they approached the end. His last
inaugural was characterized by a solemn religious tone,
peculiarly free from earthly passion. Listen to his
words : "With malice toward none, with charity for all,
with firmness in the right, as God gives us to see the
right, let us strive on to finish the work we are in, to bind
up the nation's wounds, to care for him who shall have
borne the battle, and for his widow and orphans, to do
all which may achieve and cherish a just and a lasting
peace among ourselves and with all nations."

Perhaps in no language, ancient or modern, are any
number of words found more touching and eloquent
than his speech of November 19, 1863, at the Gettysburg celebration.

He wrote it in a few moments on being told that he
would be expected to make some remarks. After
Edward Everett had delivered his masterly oration,
President Lincoln rose and read the following brief
address : —

"Fourscore and seven years ago, our fathers brought forth upon this continent a new nation, conceived in liberty, and dedicated to the proposition that all men are created equal. We are engaged in a great civil war, testing whether that nation — or any nation so conceived and so dedicated — can long endure. We are met on a great battle-field of that war. We are met to dedicate a portion of that field as the final resting-place of those who here gave their lives that that nation might live. It is altogether fitting and proper that we should do this. But, in a larger sense, we cannot dedicate, we cannot consecrate, we cannot hallow this ground. The brave men, living and dead, who struggled here, have consecrated it far above our power to add or detract. The world will little note, nor long remember, what we say here; but it can never forget what they did here.

"It is for us, the living, rather to be dedicated here to the unfinished work which they have thus far so nobly carried on. It is rather for us to be here dedicated to the great task remaining before us; that from these honored dead we take increased devotion to that cause for which they here gave the last full measure of devotion; that we here highly resolve that these dead shall not have died in vain; that this nation shall, under

God, have a new birth of freedom ; and that government of the people, by the people, for the people, shall
not perish from the earth."

The audience admired Everett's long address, but at
Mr. Lincoln's few and simple words they cheered, and
sobbed, and wept. When the President had ended, he
turned and congratulated the distinguished orator from
the Old Bay State on having succeeded so well. Mr.
Everett replied with a truthful and real compliment :
"Ah, Mr. Lincoln, how gladly would I exchange all my
hundred pages, to have been the author of your twenty
lines." Time has tested the strength of this short,
simple address. After more than a quarter of a century, its glowing words are still being committed to
memory by young people throughout our broad land.

XIX

THE BLACK REGIMENT

[*George H. Boker. Port Hudson, La., June,* 1863.]

DARK as the clouds of even,
Ranked in the western heaven,
Waiting the breath that lifts
All the dread mass, and drifts
Tempest and falling brand
Over a ruined land ; —
So still and orderly,
Arm to arm, knee to knee,
Waiting the great event,
Stands the Black Regiment.

Down the long dusky line
Teeth gleam and eyeballs shine ;
And the bright bayonet,
Bristling and firmly set,
Flashed with a purpose grand, ·
Long ere the sharp command

Of the fierce rolling drum
Told them their time had come,
Told them what work was sent
For the Black Regiment.

" Now," the flag-sergeant cried,
" Though death and hell betide,
Let the whole nation see
If we are fit to be
Free in this land ; or bound
Down, like the whining hound, —
Bound with red stripes of pain
In our old chains again ! "
Oh, what a shout there went
From the Black Regiment !

" *Charge !* "   Trump and drum awoke,
Onward the bondmen broke ;
Bayonet and sabre-stroke
Vainly oppose their rush.
Through the wild battle's crush,
With but one thought aflush,
Driving their lords like chaff,
In the guns' mouths they laugh ;
Or at the slippery brands
Leaping with open hands,

Down they tear man and horse,
Down in their awful course ;
Trampling with bloody heel
Over the crashing steel,
All their eyes forward bent,
Rushed the Black Regiment.

"Freedom !" their battle-cry —
" Freedom ! or leave to die !"
Ah ! and they meant the word,
Not as with us 'tis heard,
Not a mere party shout :
They gave their spirits out ;
Trusted the end to God,
And on the gory sod
Rolled in triumphant blood.

Glad to strike one free blow,
Whether for weal or woe ;
Glad to breathe one free breath,
Though on the lips of death.
Praying — alas ! in vain ! —
That they might fall again,
So they could once more see
That burst to liberty !
This was what "freedom " lent
To the Black Regiment.

Hundreds on hundreds fell ;
But they are resting well ;
Scourges and shackles strong
Never shall do them wrong.

Oh, to the living few,
Soldiers, be just and true !
Hail them as comrades tried ;
Fight with them side by side ;
Never, in field or tent,
Scorn the Black Regiment.

XX

TWO SCOUTS WHO HAD NERVES OF STEEL

THE scout must be a man with a cool head, resolute will, and nerves of steel.   Such a man was a scout named Hancock, attached to General Grant's army in Virginia.   He was captured as a spy and sent to Castle Thunder in Richmond.   This bold scout was remarkable for his facial expression and powers of mimicry. He was a jolly fellow, and often relieved the monotony of prison life with merry song and dances.

One evening, while singing a song for the amusement of his fellow-prisoners, he suddenly stopped, threw up his hands, staggered, and then fell like a bag of sand to the floor.

There was great confusion among the men, and as some of them inspected the body and pronounced it without life, the guards were notified of what had occurred.

The post surgeon was called in to say whether it was a faint or a case of sudden death.   It happened that he had just come in from a long, cold ride, and he was tired and in a hurry to get to his quarters, so his examination was hardly more than a look at the man.

"Dead!" he said, as he rose up, and in the course of twenty minutes the body was deposited in a wagon to be sent to the hospital, and there laid in a cheap coffin and forwarded to the burying-place.

When the driver reached the end of his journey the body was gone!

There was no tail-board to his vehicle, and, thinking he might have jolted the body out on the way, he drove back and made inquiry of several persons if they had seen a lost corpse anywhere.

Hancock's "sudden death" was a part of his plan to make an attempt to escape. While he had great nerve and an iron will, his being so quickly passed by the surgeon was a surprise to him, for he knew he could hardly have passed under less favorable circumstances.

On the way to the hospital he had dropped out of the wagon and joined the pedestrians on the walk. When the driver returned to the Castle and told his story, a detail of men was at once sent out to capture the tricky prisoner, and the alarm was given.

To leave the city was to be picked up by a patrol; to remain in it was to be hunted down. Hancock had money sewed in the lining of his vest, and he walked

straight to the best hotel, registered himself as from
Georgia, and took a good night's sleep.

In the morning he procured a change of clothing, and
sauntered around the city with the greatest unconcern,
carrying the idea to some that he was in Richmond on
a government contract, and to others that he was in the
secret service of the Confederacy.

Shortly after dinner he was arrested on Main Street
by a squad of provost troops, who had his description
to a dot. But no sooner had they put hands on him
than the prisoner was seen to be cross-eyed and to have
his mouth drawn to one side.

The men were bewildered, and Hancock was feeling
for "letters to prove his identity," when the hotel-
clerk happened to pass and at once secured his liberty.

Four days after his escape from the Castle, the scout
found himself out of money, and while in the corridor
of the post-office he was again arrested.

This time he drew his mouth to the right, brought a
squint to his left eye, and pretended to be very deaf.
He was, however, taken to the Castle, and there a wonderful thing occurred.

Guards who knew Hancock's face perfectly well were
so confused by his squint that no man dared give a certain answer.

Prisoners who had been with him for four months were equally at fault, and it was finally decided to lock him up and investigate his references.

For seven long days the scout kept his mouth twisted around and his eye on the squint, and then he got tired of it and resumed his accustomed phiz.

The minute he did this he was recognized by everybody, and the Confederates admired his nerve and perseverance fully as much as did his fellow-prisoners.

The close of the war gave him his liberty with the rest, but ten days longer would have seen him shot as a spy.

Scout number two was on the Confederate side. He is now a leading clergyman in Virginia. His life was one of daring adventure and hairbreadth escapes. Once upon a time, the house in which he was hid was surrounded by a detachment of Union soldiers. The scout took in everything at a glance and determined to try to cut his way through the soldiers and risk the chances. But the ladies represented to him that this was certain death. They could conceal him, and S—— assented.

The young ladies acted promptly. One ran to the window and asked who was there, while another closed the back door — that in front being already fastened.

S—— was then hurried up the staircase, one of the ladies accompanying him to show him his hiding-place.

The Federal troops became impatient. The door was burst in and the troopers swarmed into the house.

S—— had been conducted to a garret bare of all furniture, but some planks lay upon the sleepers of the ceiling, and by lying down on these a man might conceal himself. He mounted quietly and stretched himself at full length, and the young lady returned to the lower floor. From his perch the scout then heard all that was said in the hall beneath.

"Where is the guerilla?" exclaimed the Federal officer.

"What guerilla?" asked one of the ladies.

"The rascal S——."

"He was here, but he has gone."

"That is untrue," the officer said, "and I am not to be trifled with. I shall search this house. But first read the orders to the men," he added, turning to a sergeant.

The sergeant obeyed, and S—— distinctly overheard the reading of his death-warrant. The paper chronicled his exploits, denounced him as a guerilla and bushwhacker, and directed that he should not be taken alive.

This was not reassuring to the scout concealed under

the rafters above. It was probable that he would be discovered, in which case death would follow.

There was but one thing to do — to sell his life dearly. After ransacking every room on the first and second floors, the troops ascended to the garret. The ladies had attempted to divert their attention from it, but one of them asked, —

" What room is that up there ? "

" The garret," was the reply.

" He may be there — show the way."

" You see the way," returned the young lady. " I do not wish to go up in the dust ; it would soil my dress."

" You go before, then," said the trooper to a negro girl who had been made to carry a lighted candle, for night had come now.

The girl laughed and said, there was nobody up there, but at the order went up-stairs to the garret, followed by the troopers.

S—— heard the tramping feet, and cocked both his pistols. The light streamed into the garret, and he saw the garret filled with troopers. His discovery seemed certain. He was about to spring down and fire, when the men growled, —

" There's nothing here," and went down the stairs again.

The servant girl had saved him by a ruse. She had taken her stand directly beneath the broad plank upon which S—— was extended, and the deep shadow had concealed him. To this ruse he doubtless owed his life. An hour afterward the Federal detachment left in extreme ill-humor, and before morning S—— was miles away from the dangerous locality where he had overheard his sentence of death.

XXI

THE CLOTHES-LINE TELEGRAPH

IN the early part of 1863, when the Union army was encamped at Falmouth, and picketing the banks of the Rappahannock, the utmost tact and ingenuity were displayed by the scouts and videttes, in gaining a knowledge of contemplated movements on either side; and here, as at various other times, the shrewdness of the colored camp-followers was remarkable.

One circumstance in particular shows how quick the race is in learning the art of communicating by signals.

There came into the Union lines a negro from a farm on the other side of the river, known by the name of Dabney, who was found to possess a remarkably clear knowledge of the topography of the whole region; and he was employed as cook and body-servant at headquarters. When he first saw our system of army telegraphs, the idea interested him intensely, and he begged the operators to explain the signs to him. They did so, and found that he could understand and remember the

meaning of the various movements as well as any of
his brethren of paler hue.

Not long after, his wife, who had come with him, expressed a great anxiety to be allowed to go over to the
other side as servant to a " secesh woman," whom General Hooker was about sending over to her friends.
The request was granted. Dabney's wife went across
the Rappahannock, and in a few days was duly installed
as laundress at the headquarters of a prominent rebel
general. Dabney, her husband, on the north bank, was
soon found to be wonderfully well informed as to all the
Confederate plans. Within an hour of the time that a
movement of any kind was projected, or even discussed,
among the Confederate generals, Hooker knew all about
it. He knew which corps was moving, or about to move,
in what direction, how long they had been on the march,
and in what force ; and all this knowledge came through
Dabney, and his reports always turned out to be true.

Yet Dabney was never absent, and never talked with
scouts, and seemed to be always taken up with his
duties as cook and groom about headquarters.

How he obtained his information remained for some
time a puzzle to the Union officers. At length, upon
much solicitation, he unfolded his marvellous secret to
one of the officers.

Taking him to a point where a clear view could be obtained of Fredericksburg, he pointed out a little cabin in the suburbs near the river bank, and asked him if he saw that clothes-line with clothes hanging on it to dry. "Well," he said, "that clothes-line tells me in half an hour just what goes on at Lee's headquarters. You see my wife over there; she washes for the officers, and cooks, and waits around, and as soon as she hears about any movement or anything going on, she comes down and moves the clothes on that line so I can understand it in a minute. That there gray shirt is Longstreet; and when she takes it off it means he's gone down about Richmond. That white shirt means Hill; and when she moves it up to the west end of the line, Hill's corps has moved up-stream. That red one is Stonewall Jackson. He's down on the right now, and if he moves she will move that red shirt."

One morning Dabney came in and reported a movement over there. "But," said he, "it don't amount to anything. They are just making believe."

An officer went out to look at the clothes-line telegraph through his field-glass. There had been quite a shifting over there among the army flannels. "But how do you know but there is something in it?"

"Do you see those two blankets pinned together at the

bottom ? " said Dabney. " Yes ; but what of it ? " said
the officer. " Why, that's her way of making a fish-
trap ; and when she pins the clothes together that way,
it means that Lee is only trying to draw us into his
fish-trap."

As long as the two armies lay watching each other on
opposite sides of the stream, Dabney, with his clothes-
line telegraph, continued to be one of the prompt 'st
and most reliable of General Hooker's scouts.

XXII

COMBAT BETWEEN THE KEARSARGE AND ALABAMA

DURING the war, the Confederates, with the aid of the British ship-builders, sent out several powerful vessels which played sad havoc with American merchantmen and whalers. These vessels were furnished with the best cannon known and the most improved shells. The most famous of these privateers was the Alabama, which captured sixty-five vessels, and destroyed many million dollars' worth of property. She was built in England, and, notwithstanding the protest of the American Minister, was allowed to go to sea in July, 1862. She sailed for the Azores under the name of the 290. She was supplied with her armament and stores by another British ship, and, shortly after putting to sea, Semmes, the former captain of the privateer Sumter, appeared on deck in full uniform as her captain.

After these long years it is not easy to realize the dismay excited among our merchants by the singularly successful career of the famous Alabama. After capturing and burning many vessels, she returned to

Europe in the summer of 1864, and went into a French port.

Let me now tell you of the memorable naval contest between the United States vessel Kearsarge, Captain John A. Winslow, and the Alabama, Captain Raphael Semmes, on the morning of June 19, 1864, off Cherbourg, France, which ended the career of the famous Confederate privateer.

The Kearsarge was lying at Flushing, Holland, when a telegram came from Mr. Dayton, the American Minister in Paris, stating that the Alabama had arrived at Cherbourg. The Kearsarge immediately put to sea, and arrived at Cherbourg in quick time, taking the Alabama quite by surprise by so sudden an appearance on her track. Through the consular agent there a sort of challenge was received by Captain Winslow from Captain Semmes, the latter stating that if the Kearsarge remained off the port he would come out and fight her, and that he would not detain the vessel long.

After cruising off the port for five days, until the 19th of June, Captain Winslow, at twenty minutes after ten o'clock, descried the starry ensign of the Alabama floating in the breeze, as she came boldly out of the western entrance, under the escort of the French ironclad Couronne. The latter retired into port after sec-

ing the combatants outside of French waters. Captain
Winslow had previously had an interview with the
admiral of Cherbourg, assuring him that in the event
of an action occurring with the Alabama, the position
of the ship should be so far off shore that no question
would be advanced about the line of jurisdiction.

The Alabama came down at full speed until within a
distance of about three-quarters of a mile, when she
opened her guns on the Kearsarge. The Kearsarge
made no reply for some minutes, but ranged up nearer,
and then opened her starboard battery, fighting six guns
and leaving only one thirty-two-pounder idle. The
Alabama fought seven guns, working them with the
greatest rapidity, sending shot and shell in a constant
stream over her adversary. Both vessels used their
starboard batteries, the ships being manœuvred in a
circle about each other at a distance of from five hundred to one thousand yards. Seven complete circles
were made during the combat, which lasted a little over
one hour. At the last of the action, when the Alabama
would have made off, she was near five miles from the
shore ; and, had the combat continued from the first in
parallel lines, with her head in-shore, the line of jurisdiction would, no doubt, have been reached. From the
first, the firing of the Alabama was rapid and wild ;

towards the close of the action her firing became better. The Kearsarge gunners, who had been cautioned against firing rapidly without direct aim, were much more deliberate; and the instructions given to point the heavy guns below rather than above the water line, and clear the deck with lighter ones, was fully observed.

Captain Winslow had endeavored, with a port helm, to close in with the Alabama ; but it was not until just before the close of the action that she was in position to use grape. This was avoided, however, by the Alabama's surrender. The effect of the training of the Kearsarge's men was evident ; nearly every shot from the guns told fearfully on the Alabama, and on the seventh rotation in the circular track she winded, setting fore-trysail and two jibs, with head in-shore. Her speed was now retarded, and by winding, her port broadside was presented to the Kearsarge, with only two guns bearing, having been able to shift over but one. Captain Winslow now saw that she was at his mercy, and a few more guns, well directed, brought down her flag, though it was difficult to ascertain whether it had been hauled down or shot away ; but a white flag having been displayed over the stern, the fire of the Kearsarge was reserved.

Two minutes had not more than elapsed before the Alabama again opened fire on the Kearsarge, with the two guns on the port side. This drew Captain Winslow's fire again, and the Kearsarge was immediately steamed ahead and laid across her bows for raking. The white flag was still flying and the Kearsarge's fire was again reserved. Shortly after this, her boats were to be seen lowering, and an officer in one of them came alongside and stated that the ship had surrendered and was fast sinking. In twenty minutes from this time the Alabama went down, her mainmast, which had been shot, breaking near the head as she sunk, and her bow rising high out of the water, as her stern rapidly settled.

A few years after the war, as you will read in your text-book of history, a court of arbitration decreed that Great Britain should pay $15,500,000 to the United States for permitting the Confederate cruisers to fit out in the English ports. These claims are commonly called the Alabama claims, from the name of the Confederate vessel which did the most harm to our shipping.

XXIII

THE MESSAGE OF LIFE

[From The Youth's Companion.]

TWENTY-FIVE years ago I was one of many witnesses of a scene that left a deep impression upon my memory. The sequel of the story, which I learned some months afterward, is narrated here with the principal event.

It was in February, 1865. I was a staff-officer of a division of the Union army stationed about Winchester, Virginia. I had succeeded in getting leave of absence for twenty days. Reaching Harper's Ferry by rail after dark, I found, to my great disappointment, that the last train for the day for Baltimore had left, and that the next train would start at five o'clock on the following morning. I gave a small reminder to the negro servant at the hotel, and received his solemn promise that he would arouse me at four o'clock. It must have been two o'clock when sleep visited my weary eyes. A rude disturbance at my door awakened me, and I became dimly conscious of the voice of the negro outside.

"What is it?" I cried testily. "What do you wake me up for at this time of night?"

"'Deed, sah, Ise sorry; 'pon my honah, I is, sah! but de train hab done gone dese two hours."

It was even so. Broad daylight — seven o'clock in the morning — the train gone, and no chance to get out of Harper's Ferry till twelve more precious hours of my leave had passed — this was the unpleasant situation to which I awoke upon that dreary February morning. Breakfast over, I strolled around the queer old place merely to while away the time.

I went back to the hotel after an hour's stroll, wrote some letters, read all the newspapers I could find about the place, and shortly after eleven o'clock went out again. This time my ear was greeted with the music of a band, playing a slow march. Several soldiers were walking briskly past, and I inquired of them if there was to be a military funeral.

"No, sir," one of them replied; "not exactly. It is an execution. Two deserters from one of the artillery regiments here are to be shot up on Bolivar Heights. Here they come!"

The solemn strains of the music were heard near at hand, and the cortége moved into the street where we stood, and wound slowly up the hill. First came the

band; then General Stevenson, the military commandant of the post, and his staff ; then the guard, preceding and following an ambulance, in which were the
condemned men.   A whole regiment followed, marching
by platoons, with reversed arms, making in the whole a
spectacle than which nothing can be more solemn.

Close behind it came, as it seemed to me, the entire
population of Harper's Ferry : a motley crowd of several thousand, embracing soldiers off duty, camp-followers, negroes, and what not.   It was a raw, damp
day, not a ray of sunlight had yet penetrated the thick
clouds, and underfoot was a thin coating of snow.

The spot selected for the dreadful scene was rather
more than a mile up the heights, where a high ridge of
ground formed a barrier for bullets that might miss
their mark.   Arrived here, the troops were formed in
two large squares of one rank each, one square within
the other, with an open face towards the ridge.   Two
graves had been dug near this ridge, and a coffin was
just in the rear of each grave.   Twenty paces in front
was the firing party of six files, under a lieutenant, at
ordered arms ; the general and his staff sat on their
horses near the centre.

Outside the outer square, the great crowd of spectators stood in perfect silence.   The condemned men had

been brought from the ambulance, and each one sat on his coffin, with his open grave before him.

They were very different in their aspect. One, a man of more than forty years, showed hardly a trace of feeling in his rugged face; but the other was a mere lad of scarcely twenty, who gazed about him with a wild, restless look, as if he could not yet understand that he was about to endure the terrible punishment of his offence.

The proceedings of the court-martial were read, reciting the charges against these men, their trial, conviction, and sentence; and then the order of General Sheridan approving the sentence, "to be shot to death with musketry," and directing it to be carried into effect at twelve o'clock, noon, of this day.

A chaplain knelt by the condemned men and prayed fervently, whispered a few words in the ear of each, wrung their hands, and retired. Two soldiers stepped forward with handkerchiefs to bind the eyes of the sufferers, and I heard the officer of the firing party give the command in a low tone, —

"Attention! — shoulder — arms '"

I looked at my watch; it was a minute past twelve. The crowd outside had been so perfectly silent that a flutter and disturbance running through it at this instant fixed everybody's attention. My heart gave a great jump as I saw a mounted orderly urging his horse through the crowd, and waving a yellow envelope over his head.

The square opened for him, and he rode in and handed the envelope to the general. Those who were permitted to see that despatch read the following :

WASHINGTON, D. C., February 23, 1865.

GENERAL JOB STEVENSON, *Harper's Ferry*, — Deserters reprieved till further orders. Stop the execution.

A. LINCOLN.

The older of the two men had so thoroughly resigned himself to his fate that he seemed unable now to realize that he was saved, and he looked around him in a dazed, bewildered way.

Not so the other ; he seemed for the first time to recover his consciousness. He clasped his hands together, and burst into tears. As there was no military execution after this at Harper's Ferry, I have no doubt that the sentence of both was finally commuted.

Powerfully as my feelings had been stirred by this scene, I still suspected that the despatch had, in fact, arrived before the cortége left Harper's Ferry, and that all that happened afterward was planned and intended as a terrible lesson to these culprits.

That afternoon I visited General Stevenson at his headquarters, and, after introducing myself and referring to the morning's scene, I ventured frankly to state my suspicions, and ask if they were not well founded.

"Not at all," he instantly replied. "The men would have been dead had that despatch reached me two minutes later. In order to give the fellows every possible chance for their lives, I left a mounted orderly at the telegraph office, with orders to ride at a gallop if a message came for me from Washington. It is well I did! — the precaution saved their lives."

How the despatch came to Harper's Ferry must be told in the words of the man who got it through.

THE TELEGRAPHER'S STORY.

On the morning of the 24th of February, 1865, I was busy at my work in the Baltimore telegraph office, sending and receiving messages. At half-past ten o'clock — for I had occasion to mark the hour — the signal C — A — L., several times repeated, caused me to throw all else aside and attend to it.

That was the telegraphic cipher of the War Department; and telegraphers, in those days, had instructions to put that service above all others. A message was quickly ticked off from the President to the commanding officer at Harper's Ferry, reprieving two deserters who were to be shot at noon. The message was dated the day before, but had in some way been detained or delayed between the Department and the Washington office.

A few words to the Baltimore office, which accompanied the despatch, explained that it had "stuck" at Baltimore, that an officer direct from the President was waiting at the Washington office, anxious to hear that it had reached Harper's Ferry, and that Baltimore must send it on instantly.

Baltimore would have been very glad to comply; but the line to Harper's Ferry had been interrupted since daylight; nothing whatever had passed. So I explained to Washington.

The reply came back before my fingers had left the instrument. "You *must* get it through. Do it, some way, for Mr. Lincoln. He is very anxious; has just sent another messenger to us."

I called the office superintendent to my table, and repeated these despatches to him. He looked at the clock.

"Almost eleven," he said. "I see just one chance — a very slight one. Send it to New York: ask them to get it to Wheeling, and then it may get through by

Cumberland and Martinsburg. Stick to 'em, and do what you can."

By this time I had become thoroughly aroused in the business, and I set to work with a will. The despatch with the explanation went to New York, and promptly came the reply that it was hopeless; the wires were crowded, and nothing could be done till late in the afternoon, if then.

I responded just as Washington had replied to me: It *must* be done; it is a case of life and death; do it for Mr. Lincoln's sake, who is very anxious about it. And I added for myself, by way of emphasis: For God's sake, let's save these poor fellows!

And I got the New-York people thoroughly aroused, as I was myself. The answer came back, "Will do what we can."

It was now ten minutes past eleven. In ten minutes more I heard from New York that the despatch had got as far as Buffalo, and could not go direct to Wheeling; it must go on to Chicago.

Inquiries from Washington were repeated every five minutes, and I sent what had reached me.

Half-past eleven, the despatch was at Chicago, and they were working their best to get it to Wheeling.

Something was the matter; the Wheeling office did not answer.

The next five minutes passed without a word; then --- huzza! — New York says the despatch has reached Wheeling, and the operator there says he can get it through to Harper's Ferry in time.

At this point the news stopped. New York could learn nothing further for me, after several efforts, and I could only send to Washington that I hoped it was all right, but could not be sure. Later in the day the line was working again to Harper's Ferry, and then I learned that the despatch had reached the office there at ten minutes before twelve, and that it was brought to the place of execution just in time.

XXIV

SHERMAN STARTS ON HIS MARCH TO THE SEA

[*From General Sherman's "Personal Memoirs."*]

ABOUT seven o'clock, on the morning of November
16, 1864, we rode out of Atlanta by the Decatur road,

WILLIAM T. SHERMAN.

filled by the marching
troops and wagons of the
Fourteenth Corps; and
reaching the hill, just outside of the old Confederate
works, we naturally paused
to look back upon the
scenes of our last battles.
We stood upon the very
ground where was fought
the bloody battle of July
22, and could see the copse
of wood where McPherson fell. Behind us lay Atlanta,
smouldering and in ruins, the black smoke rising high in
the air, and hanging like a pall over the city. Away off
in the distance, on the McDonough road, was the rear

SHERMAN'S ARMY FORAGING.

of Howard's column, the gun-barrels glistening in the sun, the white-topped wagons stretching away to the south; and right before us the Fourteenth Corps, marching steadily and rapidly with a cheery look and swinging pace, that made light of the thousand miles that lay between us and Richmond. Some band, by accident, struck up the anthem of "John Brown's soul goes marching on," the men caught up the strain, and never, before or since, have I heard the chorus of "Glory, glory, hallelujah!" done with more spirit, or in better harmony of time and place.

Then we turned our horses' heads to the east. Atlanta was soon lost behind the screen of trees, and became a thing of the past. Around it clings many a thought of desperate battle, of hope and fear, that now seems like the memory of a dream; and I have never seen the place since. The day was extremely beautiful, clear sunlight, with bracing air; and an unusual feeling of exhilaration seemed to pervade all minds, a feeling of something to come, vague and undefined, still full of venture and intense interest. Even the common soldiers caught the inspiration, and many a group called out to me as I worked my way past them, "Uncle Billy, I guess Grant is waiting for us at Richmond!" Indeed the general sentiment was that we were march-

ing for Richmond, and that there we should end the
war; but how and when they seemed to care not, nor
did they measure the distance, or count the cost in life,
or bother their brains about the great rivers to be
crossed, and the food required for man and beast, that
had to be gathered by the way. There was a "devil-
may-care" feeling pervading officers and men, that
made me feel the full load of responsibility, for success
would be accepted as a matter of course, whereas,
should we fail, this "march" would be adjudged the
wild adventure of a crazy fool. I had no purpose to
march direct for Richmond by way of Augusta and
Charlotte, but always designed to reach the seacoast
first at Savannah or Port Royal, South Carolina, and
even kept in mind the alternative of Pensacola.

The first night out we camped by the roadside.
Stone Mountain, a mass of granite, was in plain view
cut out in clear outline against the blue sky; the whole
horizon was lurid with the bonfires of rail-ties, and
groups of men all night were carrying the heated rails
to the nearest trees and bending them around the
trunks. Colonel Poe had provided tools for ripping up
the rails and twisting them when hot; but the best and
easiest way is the one I have described, of heating the
middle of the iron rails on bonfires made of the cross-

ties, and then winding them around a telegraph-pole or the trunk of some convenient sapling. I attached much importance to this destruction of the railroad, gave it my own personal attention, and made reiterated orders to others on the subject.

The next day we passed through the handsome town of Covington, the soldiers closing up their ranks, the color-bearers unfurling their flags, and the bands striking up patriotic airs. The white people came out of their houses to behold the sight, spite of their deep hatred of the invaders, and the negroes were simply frantic with joy. Whenever they heard my name, they clustered about my horse, shouted and prayed in their peculiar style, which had a natural eloquence that would have moved a stone. I have witnessed hundreds, if not thousands, of such scenes, and can now see a poor girl, in the very ecstasy of hugging the banner of one of the regiments.

I remember, when riding around by a by-street in Covington to avoid the crowd that followed the marching column, that some one brought me an invitation to dine with a sister of Sam Anderson, who was a cadet at West Point with me ; but the messenger reached me after we had passed the main part of the town. I asked to be excused, and rode on to a place designated

for camp about four miles to the east of the town.
Here we made our bivouac, and I walked up to a plan-
tation-house close by, where were assembled many
negroes, among them an old, gray-haired man, with as
fine a head as I ever saw. I asked him if he understood about the war and its progress. He said he did ;
that he had been looking for the "angel of the Lord"
ever since he was knee-high, and, though we professed
to be fighting for the Union, he supposed that slavery
was the cause, and that our success was his freedom.
I asked him if all the negro slaves comprehended this
fact, and he said they did surely. I then explained
to him that we wanted the slaves to remain where they
were and not to load us down with useless mouths,
which would eat up the food needed for our fighting
men ; that our success was their assured freedom ; that
we could receive a few of their young, hearty men as
pioneers ; but that, if they followed us in swarms of old
and young, feeble and helpless, it would simply load us
down and cripple us in our great task. I believe that
old man spread this message to the slaves, which was
carried from mouth to mouth, to the very end of our
journey, and that in part saved us from the great danger we incurred of swelling our numbers so that famine
would have attended our progress. It was at this very

ON THE MARCH TO THE SEA.

plantation that a soldier passed me with a ham on his musket, a jug of sorghum molasses under his arm, and a big piece of honey in his hand, from which he was eating, and, catching my eye, he remarked *sotto voce* and carelessly to a comrade, " Forage liberally on the country," quoting from my general orders. On this occasion, as on many others that fell under my personal observation, I reproved the man, explained that foraging must be limited to the regular parties properly detailed, and that all provisions thus obtained must be delivered to the regular commissaries to be fairly distributed to the men who kept their ranks.

XXV

SHERMAN'S MARCH TO THE SEA

[*By Samuel H. M. Byers.*]

[THIS popular song was written while its author was a prisoner at Columbia, S. C. Of its origin he says: " There are hundreds of old comrades who remember the afternoon in the prison-pen at Columbia when our glee club said, ' Now we are going to sing something about Billy Sherman!' and with what rousing cheers the song and the writer were welcomed. The Confederate officers ran in to see what was loose among the prisoners, and they, too, had music in their souls, and said if the glee club would sing ' Dixie Land' they might sing 'Sherman's March to the Sea' also; and so for weeks our glee club — the only sunshine we had in prison — made the old barrack walls ring with songs of the blue and the gray."]

OUR campfires shone bright on the mountain
  That frowned on the river below,
As we stood by our guns in the morning,
  And eagerly watched for the foe ;
When a rider came out of the darkness
  That hung over mountain and tree,
And shouted, " Boys, up and be ready !
  For Sherman will march to the sea ! "

Then cheer upon cheer for bold Sherman
  Went up from each valley and glen,
And the bugles re-echoed the music
  That came from the lips of the men ;
For we knew that the stars in our banner
  More bright in their splendor would be,
And that blessings from Northland would greet us
  When Sherman marched down to the sea.

Then forward, boys! forward to battle!
We marched on our wearisome way,
We stormed the wild hills of Resaca —
God bless those who fell on that day!
Then Kenesaw, dark in its glory,
Frowned down on the flag of the free;
But the East and the West bore our standard,
And Sherman marched on to the sea.

Still onward we pressed, till our banners
Swept out from Atlanta's grim walls,
And the blood of the patriot dampened
The soil where the traitor flag falls;
We paused not to weep for the fallen
Who slept by each river and tree,
Yet we twined them a wreath of the laurel,
As Sherman marched down to the sea.

Oh, proud was our army that morning,
That stood where the pine darkly towers,
When Sherman said, "Boys, you are weary,
But to-day fair Savannah is ours!"
Then sang we the song of our chieftain,
That echoed o'er river and lea,
And the stars in our banner shone brighter
When Sherman marched down to the sea.

XXVI

THE PERILS OF A SPY'S LIFE

THE life of a spy is one full of peril and hardship. The danger incurred is often more serious and personal than that of the battle-field. He is sent by his superiors to discover, if possible, the enemy's plans, in order to thwart them. The spy goes to his duty fully aware of the possibilities in store for him. If the enemy catches him, he knows that in a few hours his dead body will dangle from a tree. Listen to the story of the narrow escape of one of the most daring spies of the Army of the Potomac.

"It was a dark night. Not a star on the glimmer. I had collected my bits of intelligence, and was on the move for the Union lines. I was approaching the banks of a stream whose waters I had to cross, and had then some miles to traverse before I could reach the pickets of our gallant troops. A feeling of uneasiness began to creep over me ; I was on the outskirt of a wood fringing the dark waters at my feet, whose presence could scarcely be detected but for their sullen murmurs as they rushed through the gloom. The wind sighed in gentle accordance. I walked forty or fifty yards along the bank. I then crept on all fours along the ground, and groped with my hands. I paused — I groped again — my breath thickened, perspiration oozed from me at every pore, and I was prostrated with horror! I had missed my landmark, and knew not where I was. Below or above, beneath the shelter of the bank, lay the skiff I had hidden ten days before.

"As I stood gasping for breath, with all the unmistakable proofs of my calling about me, the sudden cry of a bird or plunging of a fish would act like magnetism on my frame, not wont to shudder at a shadow. No matter how pressing the danger may be, if a man sees an opportunity for escape, he breathes with freedom. But let him be surrounded by darkness, impenetrable at two yards' distance, within rifle's length of concealed foes, for what knowledge he has to the contrary; knowing, too, with painful accuracy, the detection of his presence would reward him with a sudden and violent death; and if he breathes no faster, and feels his limbs as free and his spirits as light as when taking a favorite promenade, he is more fitted for a hero than I am.

"In the agony of that moment — in the sudden and

utter helplessness I felt to discover my true bearings —
I was about to let myself gently into the stream, and
breast its current, for life or death. There was no
alternative. The Union pickets must be reached in
safety before the morning broke, or I should soon
swing between heaven and earth, from some green limb
of the black forest in which I stood.

"At that moment the low, sullen bay of a blood-
hound struck my ear. The sound was reviving — the
fearful stillness broken. The uncertain dread flew
before the certain danger. I was standing to my
middle in the shallow bed of the river, just beneath the
jutting banks. After a pause of a few seconds I began
to creep mechanically and stealthily down the stream,
followed, as I knew from the rustling of the grass and
frequent breaking of twigs, by the bloodthirsty dog;
although, by certain uneasy growls, I felt assured he
was at fault. Something struck against my breast. I
could not prevent a slight cry from escaping me, as,
stretching out my hand, I grasped the gunwale of a boat
moored beneath the bank. Between surprise and joy I
felt half choked. In an instant I had scrambled on
board, and began to search for the painter in the bow,
in order to cast her from her fastenings.

"Suddenly, a bright ray of moonlight — the first

gleam of hope in that black night — fell directly on the
spot, revealing the silvery stream, my own skiff (hidden
there ten days before), lighting the deep shadows of the
verging wood, and, on the log half buried in the bank,
and from which I had that instant cast the line that had
bound me to it, the supple form of the crouching blood-
hound, his red eyes gleaming in the moonlight, jaws
distended, and poising for the spring. With one dart
the light skiff was yards out in the stream, and the
savage after it. With an oar I aimed a blow at his head,
which, however, he eluded with ease. In the effort thus
made the boat careened over towards my antagonist,
who made a desperate effort to get his forepaws over
the side, at the same time seizing the gunwale with his
teeth.

"Now was the time to get rid of my canine foe.
I drew my revolver, and placed the muzzle between his
eyes, but hesitated to fire, for that one report might
bring on me a volley from the shore. Meantime, the
strength of the dog careened the frail craft so much
that the water rushed over the side, threatening to
swamp her. I changed my tactics, threw my revolver
into the bottom of the skiff, and, grasping my 'bowie,'
keen as a Malay creese, and glittering, as I released it
from the sheath, like a moonbeam on the stream, in

an instant I had severed the sinewy throat of the hound, cutting through brawn and muscle to the nape of the neck. The tenacious wretch gave a wild, convulsive leap half out of the water, then sank, and was gone.

"Five minutes' pulling landed me on the other side of the river, and in an hour after, without further accident, I was among friends, encompassed by the Union lines. That night I related at headquarters the intelligence I had gathered."

Not often does the spy escape from his enemies so easily. A staff officer thus describes the death of a spy, who had been caught by one of General Custer's officers in a village near Cedar Creek, Virginia:

"'What's the matter?' said I to Custer, who was sitting with his staff round the campfire. 'You seem sad.'

"'I have reason to be. I fear we have a disagreeable duty to perform. You know we captured a man in the village.'

"'Yes. What of him?'

"'Only that my adjutant-general has just recognized him as one of the Confederate guards who escorted him and other Federals when they were taken prisoners. He has gone with two other officers, who were captured at the same time, to see the prisoner.'

"'You think, then, the fellow is a spy?'

"'That's just it; and a dangerous one, too, judging from his looks.'

"At that moment the three officers came up to make their report.

"'Well, gentlemen,' said Custer, 'what do you think of the prisoner?'

"'We all recognized him as one of our old guards,' said the adjutant.

"'Very well, gentlemen,' said Custer slowly. 'The evidence seems to be clear. Adjutant, order the prisoner to be brought before me.'

"The prisoner was brought up between two sentries. 'My man, we think you are a spy,' said General Custer, in a quiet voice. 'What have you to say to the charge?'

"'There's a woman here from the village,' replied the man, 'and she'll tell you I am her son. I live in the village. Does that make me a spy?'

"An elderly woman, evidently in some terror, came forward.

"'Is this man your son?'

"'Yes, he is.'

"'How long has he been in the village?'

"'Ever since last spring.'

"'Does he belong to the Southern army?'

"'I dunno.'

"At this moment an orderly handed the adjutant-general a bundle, and whispered a word in his ear. Quietly unrolling it, the adjutant brought out a Confederate uniform.

"'General,' said he, 'this uniform was found in the woman's house where we captured the prisoner.'

"A sudden flash in the man's face, a swift look of anger, and a glance between him and the woman was the only answer either made to the announcement.

"'That will do; remove the woman,' said Custer gravely.

"The woman gazed for a moment into the face of the prisoner, but it was evident that she was not his mother. She made no effort to bid him farewell.

"'My man, it's a clear case. You are a soldier of the Confederate army, and inside our lines in disguise. You are therefore a spy. It is my duty to inform you that you must die.'

"'Die? What! without a trial?' exclaimed the startled prisoner.

"'You have just been tried. I, as a United States general, have condemned you as a spy. You die at

eight to-morrow morning. I will send the chaplain to
you, and I hope you will prepare to meet your fate.'

"At the appointed hour the next morning the poor
fellow was brought out and hanged, in the presence of
the entire brigade."

XXVII

HOW ADMIRAL FARRAGUT WAS LASHED TO THE RIGGING

SOME day you will read all about the brilliant naval fight for the possession of Mobile Bay. The brave

DAVID G. FARRAGUT.

Admiral Farragut had determined to make the attempt on Thursday, August 4, 1864, but was delayed because one of his ironclads did not arrive. The vessel arrived at sunset, and Farragut gave orders for the fleet to move at sunrise. The day opened with a dense fog which hid the forts in the bay, and made the great men-of-war and black ironclads look like so many phantoms. The fog soon lifted, and at an early hour the whole fleet was under way. Now was fought one of the most brilliant naval contests of modern times. By this victory the port of Mobile was closed against blockade-runners.

During the fight an incident happened which caught the public fancy at the time, and has since become fixed in the popular mind as an incident of deep historical interest for all time.

At the beginning of the action, Admiral Farragut was standing in the main port rigging, which position enabled him to overlook the other vessels of the fleet. It also gave him command of both his own flagship and the Metacomet. The latter vessel was lashed on to the port side of the Hartford, for the purpose of carrying the flagship inside the bay in case her machinery should be disabled. A slight breeze was blowing the smoke from the Union guns on to Fort Morgan. Soon the smoke gradually obscured the admiral's view, and he almost unconsciously climbed the rigging, ratline by ratline, in order to see over it, until finally he found himself in shrouds, some little distance below the main-top. Here he could lean either backward or for-ward in a comfortable position, having the free use of both hands for his spyglass, or any other purpose. Captain Drayton, commanding the Hartford, also chief of staff to the admiral, becoming anxious lest even a slight wound, a blow from a splinter, or the cutting away of a portion of the rigging, might throw his chief to the deck, sent the signal-quartermaster aloft with a small rope to secure him to the rigging. The admiral at first declined to allow the quartermaster to do this, but quickly admitted the wisdom of the precaution, and himself passed two or three turns of the rope around his body. The admiral remained aloft until after the flagship had passed Fort Morgan.

After the passage of the forts was accomplished and the vessels were anchored, the Confederate ram Tennessee was seen to be moving out from under the guns of Fort Morgan. Captain Drayton reported this fact to the admiral, stating that Buchanan, the Confederate admiral, was going outside to destroy the outer fleet. The admiral immediately said, "Then we must follow him out!" though he suspected that Buchanan, becoming desperate, had made up his mind to sink or destroy the flagship Hartford, and do as much injury as possible before losing his own vessel. Soon after this remark, Farragut said, "No! Buck's coming here. Get under way at once; we must be ready for him."

Of the desperate fight which now took place we may learn more details at some future time. After a fierce contest, the great ram, the pride and boast of the Confederate navy, and under the command of Buchanan,

FARRAGUT LASHED TO THE RIGGING

the commander of the Merrimac in the fight with the Monitor, was forced to surrender.

The fact that the admiral was lashed in the main rigging during the fight gave him a great reputation throughout the country. Farragut was amused and amazed at the notoriety of the incident. When a comic picture of the scene, in one of the illustrated papers, came to hand a few days after the battle, the admiral said to Captain Drayton in conversation, "How curiously some trifling incident catches the popular fancy. My being in the main rigging was a mere incident, owing to the fact that I was driven aloft by the smoke. The lashing was the result of your own fears for my safety." At the close of the war the admiral yielded to the solicitations of a celebrated artist, to stand for a historical portrait in the position in which he was first lashed.

XXVIII

THE HORRORS OF ANDERSONVILLE PRISON

[From Warren Lee Goss's "Jed."]

THE rain was pouring in torrents when, on the 23d of May, 1864, about sundown, we arrived at Anderson Station. We were formed in single ranks on the long platform of the depot, and were then formally turned over to the prison guard. We were marched east a short distance, by a road running through a little valley, surrounded by thick pine woods, when there loomed up before us, in the moist atmosphere and gathering darkness, a long line of palisades, the sight of which gave me a shiver of foreboding and dread. The rainfall and the chill of evening oppressed me with gloom.

The gates before us now swung inward, and we were marched into the prison. Many, oh, how many! never passed through those gates again until they were carried to the graveyard trenches beyond. Gaunt creatures, with shrunken forms and blackened faces, clothed in dirty, ragged shreds of blue, thronged round us as

we entered the prison. The impress of suffering and
famine was over all. Their hollow-eyed countenances,
dishevelled hair, half-naked limbs, and grotesque habili-
ments, for a while made it impossible for us to realize
that they, like ourselves, were Union soldiers.

Exposure to rain and sun, starvation and confinement
within the deadly embrace of these prison walls had
obliterated all semblance of manhood from these
patriotic men. Some stared apathetically at us, as if
visitants from another world, in which they no longer
had a part. From their faces all hope and cheerfulness
had faded out. Others gathered around us, and in
plaintive, tremulous, but eager voices, inquired for news
of the outside world from where we came, or invited
to trade. "Where is Sherman?" "What is Grant
doing?" "Got any hard-tack or coffee to trade for
corn bread?" "Do you know when we are to be exchanged?" are samples of the interrogations which
came from faltering lips. The last question was the
most common one. This, coming from wretched men,
hollow-eyed, famine-pinched, and with scurvied, swol-
len faces, blue and trembling with cold, dampness, and
the weakness of famine, made the questionings almost
an appeal. Though this scene brought a shiver of
creeping horror over many a man among us accustomed

to face death in battle, yet we but feebly comprehended its full import then.

A revolting stench filled the moist atmosphere. Our feet mired into a wallow of filth at every step. We constantly stumbled on squalid huts scarcely high enough to creep under. These were made of blankets, shirts, shreds of clothing, or were built up with mud and roofed with brush or twigs of pine. Coming from ordinary scenes of war, this prison, by contrast, was so horrible as to seem to be the very jaws of death and the gates of hell. Within its deadly maw all semblance of humanity was crushed.

The side hill beyond, we were told, was to be our quarters. But where? The whole hillside was so crowded with huts and human forms lying on the muddy ground, that at a first glance there appeared to be no room for us. It was only by scattering in groups of two or three at different points that we finally found the needed space to spread our blankets.

Sadly thinking of my far-off Northern home and friends, and of the terrible contrasts here, I fell into a troubled sleep. The sun was shining brightly when I was awakened by men stumbling against me. As I arose to my feet the daylight revealed, for the first time, the whole prison area to my sight.

In form the enclosure of stockade was a parallelogram, shown by after measurements to be ten hundred
and ten feet in length, and seven hundred and seventy-
nine feet wide. The sides of this parallelogram ran
north and south. It enclosed two opposite hillsides,
and the valleys and plateaus back of them. Near the
centre, running from east to west, was a brook, eight to
ten feet in width. On each side of this creek was a
swampy marsh reaching to the foot of both the north
and south hillsides.

The stockade was built of pine logs set upright in the
ground, scored slightly on the sides, so as to fit them
closely together. These were firmly held together by
means of a plank or slab, spiked on the outside and
across the face of the logs near the top. Sentry
boxes, thirty-five in number, were scaffolded outside,
close to the stockade, so that the guard could overlook the area within.

No vegetation was in this pen. The dense growth
of pines formerly covering the ground had been cleared
away when the stockade was built.

As I went down the hill to wash myself at the brook
I saw, for the first time, a little railing three feet high,
running eighteen feet from, and parallel with, the
stockade, inside and all around it. It was made by

nailing a strip of board, about three inches wide, to the top of posts set firmly in the ground.

"What is that for?" I asked an old prisoner.

"You'd better keep away from it if you don't want to get shot," he replied. "That's the dead line. I saw one of the guard shoot one of our old men the other day while he was reaching over to pick up a weed which was growing inside."

"What did he want of the weed?" I inquired wonderingly.

"Don't know. Guess he wanted it to eat; good for scurvy," was the reply.

On every side strange and terrible sights greeted me. Men were cooking at little fires scarcely large enough to make a blaze. Dead men, with unclosed eyes, lay in the path by the side of the little huts. Sick men, with scurvied, bloated limbs, were trying to eat, while their teeth almost dropped from their jaws. Wounded men, with festering, unhealed wounds, were lying with naked limbs and with hair matted in the filth of their surroundings.

With inarticulate, piteous whines, they looked with their lustreless eyes or reached out their withered, feeble hands in mute appeal for help. They were covered with vermin. God in heaven! what horrors greeted every step!

Such was our introduction to the living death of Andersonville, and thus it was that we settled down to the common life of prisoners. As bitter and terrible as was the opening scene described, it afterwards became inexpressibly worse, month by month, during our stay there.

XXIX

THE HEROISM OF REBECCA WRIGHT

[From General Sheridan's "Personal Memoirs"]

EARLY in the fall of 1864, I felt the need of an efficient body of scouts to collect information concerning the enemy. I therefore began to organize my scouts on a system which I hoped would give better results than had the method hitherto pursued in the department, which was to employ doubtful citizens and Confederate deserters. If these should turn out untrustworthy, the mischief they might do us gave me grave apprehensions. I finally concluded that those of our own soldiers who should volunteer for the delicate and hazardous duty would be the most valuable material. These men were disguised in Confederate uniforms whenever necessary, were paid from the secret-service fund in proportion to the value of the intelligence they furnished, which often stood us in good stead in checking the forays of Harry Gilmor, Mosby, and other irregulars.

Beneficial results came from the plan in many other

ways too, and particularly so when, in a few days, two
of my scouts put me in the way of getting news conveyed from Winchester. They had learned that just
outside of my lines there was living an old colored man
who had a permit from the Confederate commander to
go into Winchester and return three times a week, for
the purpose of selling vegetables to the inhabitants.
The scouts had sounded this man, and, finding him both
loyal and shrewd, suggested that he might be made
useful to us within the enemy's lines. The proposal
struck me as feasible, provided there could be found in
Winchester some trustworthy person who would be willing to co-operate and correspond with me. I asked
General Crook, who was acquainted with many of the
Union people of Winchester, if he knew of such a person, and he recommended a Miss Rebecca Wright, a
young lady whom he had met there before the battle of
Kernstown, who, he said, was a member of the Society
of Friends and the teacher of a small private school.
He knew she was faithful and loyal to the government,
and thought she might be willing to render us assistance ; but he could not be certain of this, for, on account of her well-known loyalty, she was under constant
surveillance. I hesitated at first, but, finally deciding to
try it, despatched the two scouts to the old negro's

cabin, and they brought him to my headquarters late at night. I was soon convinced of the negro's fidelity, and, asking him if he was acquainted with Miss Rebecca Wright of Winchester, he replied that he knew her well. Thereupon, I told him what I wished to do, and, after a little persuasion, he agreed to carry a letter to the young lady on his next marketing trip.

My message was prepared by writing it on tissue paper, which was then compressed into a small pellet, and protected by wrapping it in tinfoil so that it could be safely carried in the man's mouth. The probability of his being searched when he came to the Confederate picket-line was not remote, and in such event he was to swallow the pellet. The letter appealed to Miss Wright's loyalty and patriotism, and requested her to furnish me with information regarding the strength and condition of Early's army. The night before the negro started, one of the scouts placed the odd-looking communication in his hands, with renewed injunctions as to secrecy and promptitude.

Early in the morning it was delivered to Miss Wright with an intimation that a letter of importance was enclosed in the tinfoil, the negro telling her at the same time that she might expect him to call for a message in

reply before his return home. At first Miss Wright
began to open the pellet nervously, but when told to be
careful, and to preserve the foil as a wrapping for her
answer, she proceeded slowly and carefully, and when
the note appeared intact the messenger retired, remark-
ing again that in the evening he would come for an
answer.

On reading my communication Miss Wright was
much startled by the perils it involved, and hesitatingly
consulted her mother; but her devoted loyalty soon
silenced every other consideration, and the brave girl
resolved to comply with my request, notwithstanding it
might jeopardize her life. The evening before, a con-
valescent Confederate officer had visited her mother's
house, and in conversation about the war had disclosed
the fact that Kershaw's division of infantry and a
battalion of artillery had started to rejoin General Lee.
At the time Miss Wright heard this, she attached but
little importance to it, but now she perceived the value
of the intelligence. As her first venture, she determined to send it to me at once, which she did, with a
promise that in the future she would with great pleasure continue to transmit information by the negro
messenger.

Miss Wright's answer proved of more value to me

than she anticipated, for it not only quieted the conflicting reports concerning Anderson's corps, but was most important in showing positively that Kershaw had gone. This circumstance led, three days later, to the battle of Winchester.

XXX

THE FORTUNES OF WAR

[From the "Youth's Companion."]

THE tide of war penetrated for the first time into Kentucky in the summer of 1862. The armed neutrality which the State had declared as its policy, and which it had striven to maintain, had proved a failure. The Confederates entered the State, hoping and expecting to find her ready to come at their call.

The attempt proved a failure. After many defeats, the broken and routed army was driven back into the valley of East Tennessee.

The silence of the forest was broken by the tramp of thousands of feet; the hills swarmed with the blue and the gray. Giant trees, the growth of centuries, were felled to make room for batteries and rifle-pits. The scanty crops of corn and potatoes were soon exhausted, and forage for man and beast became every day more scarce.

Supplies were brought up the river on steamboats, then transferred to wagon-trains, and, when the roads became impassable, were carried on pack mules.

So the advancing Federal army under Burnside had no lack. But for General Bragg's men, who were retreating, weary, discouraged, footsore and ragged, there was no recourse but to ravage the surrounding country, and this they did with such effect that the natives, who are always abjectly poor, were reduced to extremities.

Communication with home was cut off, and mails were irregular and infrequent. Yet it was a question whether to be glad or to be sorry when a mail did come, so piteous were the tales of destitution and need that it brought.

The early twilight was settling down, a light fall of snow had sprinkled the hills with white, the wind whistled drearily through the pine trees. Shivering, the men drew closer to the roaring campfire.

Suddenly one of the group started up, and, dashing a letter he had been reading to the ground, exclaimed, "Boys, I'm bound ter git a leave an' go home fur a week!"

"Git a leave in the face uv the Blue Jackets! Why, John Rowsey, air ye crazy?"

"I tell yer, fellers, I'm bound ter go — my wife an' the young uns they's starvin', ain't got nothing to eat at all!"

He groaned as he walked away to present his petition to General Breckinridge, his brigade commander.

With orderlies and adjutants on guard, it is by no means easy for a private to approach his chief, but a motive such as impelled Rowsey would have overcome even greater obstacles than these, and he was in a short time standing in the general's tent.

"Beg pardon, general," said the aide, "I tried to keep the man out, but nothing would do but he must see you himself."

The young officers who filled the tent smiled audibly at the appearance of the ragged, unkempt, shoeless man who presented himself among them. But General Breckinridge was too polite to find matter for merriment in genuine distress, however humble. With a glance of stern rebuke to the jesters, he turned, and, with the same gracious, sweet courtesy that marked his manners to every one, he said, "Well, my man, what can I do for you?"

"I would like a week's leave, general, if you please."

"Why, my good fellow, don't you know that in the face of the enemy no one can have a leave?"

"Read that, general, if you please."

It was a torn and soiled half-sheet of coarse paper.

The general took it, and these were the pencilled words he deciphered :

DEAR JOHN, — Can't you come home and help us? We ain't had nothin' ter eat sence day before yesterday, 'cep' some dry crusts uv corn bread. The soldiers hev took everything. They've kilt the cow, an' the meal's all gone ; if you can't come soon we'll all be starved. Good-by, an' God bless you if I don't see you no more.   MARY.

No petition from high official had ever moved General Breckinridge as did that simple little letter.

"My poor fellow," said he, laying his hand on the soldier's shoulder, " I will indorse your petition and send it up to headquarters. You know that when we are so near a battle as now no one but the commanding general can grant a leave, but you shall have it if I can get it for you."

" God bless you, general!" sobbed the poor fellow, as he sank on his knees. "God bless you, and thank you kindly."

There were few dry eyes in the tent as Breckinridge read the letter to the officers who surrounded him, after Rowsey had gone, and he lost no time in sending it with his own indorsement to General Bragg.

John Rowsey slept with troubled dreams of love and Mary, and awoke stretching out his arms and crying, "I'm a-coming, Mary, I'm coming !"

"Pore feller," said his comrades, "he's all dazed wi' his trouble."

"Message for Private John Rowsey, Company E, —th, K. V. M.," called out a gay-looking officer, galloping down the line.

Flushed with hope, he came forward, received the packet, and tore it open eagerly; but when he saw his wife's letter enclosed with General Breckinridge's indorsement, while across the paper were written the fatal words, "Request disallowed," he dropped heavily to the ground. "I tell yer, boys, I must go!" he said an hour or two later to a group of friends.

"But yer'll be caught!"

"Ef I am they can't do nothin' but shoot me, an' I rather be dead than stay here. Good Lord, you dunno what 'tis ter feel as them as yer love better'n yerself's starvin' ter death, an' you can't do nothin' ter help 'em!"

After that no one said anything to hinder him, but all gave him money to help him.

"Give my respects to General Breckinridge, Jim," he said to a comrade, as he started, "an' thank him fur what he tried to do fur me, an' tell him I hed ter go." Then he turned and walked quietly down the line, into the thick woods patrolled by the boys in gray.

Past the first and second sentry he went unchallenged, no one taking notice of the man who walked along coolly and seemed to be minding his business. Only one more picket, and then — freedom and Mary, when —

"Who goes there?" called a stentorian voice.

"A friend."

"Advance and give the countersign."

A dash through the woods was the only answer. What odds, however, had one against half a dozen? The sentry's gun gave the alarm, and John Rowsey was surrounded and lodged in the guard-house.

The tidings soon penetrated to the little group who were so anxiously awaiting the result.

"Sarves him right," said a burly Tennessean, "fur desartin' his country's flag."

"Shet up, Jake Larkins! Country's well enough, but if them what's bone o' yer bone's a-starvin' an' a-callin' fur ye, I reckon ye wouldn't be thinking 'bout country," said Jim, as he strode off to Breckinridge's quarters.

"Is it any use, general, do ye think, axin' fur a pardon? I knows as it's a mighty bad case, but jes' ye think what was pullin' the poor feller t'other way."

"I'll see, I'll see," said the general, with a tremble in his voice.

" My God, I wish I had given him the leave and taken the risk myself."

And "see" he did, for he got up a petition which was signed by half a dozen brigade commanders; but all to no effect.

"Deserter John Rowsey to be shot at high noon," was the sentence issued.

The prisoner sat in the guard-house trying to write a letter by a dim light. As he was writing, General Breckenridge opened the door and came in.

"My poor fellow, I am sorry for this!"

" I knowed you'd be, general, I knowed you'd be. I love my country, too, but I couldn't help doin' it. I was bound to go, you see."

" Is there anything I can do for you?"

"If you'd find my Mary, general, an' tell her how I tried ter come, an' give her this letter, an' if you could help her a bit."

"I will, I will," was the answer. "I will find her myself."

"An', general, you don't think I run away cos I was a coward?"

"A coward, no!" and the kindly blue eyes shone with moisture.

"I ain't afeard ter fight, an' I ain't afeard ter

die, but there's some things as takes the heart outer a feller."

"I'll tell Mary that you died like a brave man," said the general, as he grasped the horny hand of the soldier.

"Bless you fur that word!" cried the other, springing up eagerly. "An' God bless you now an' alwiz, an keep you frum trouble like mine!" And there they stood hand in hand, the general and the gentleman, and the uncouth mountaineer whose ideas were limited to his native hills.

Around a large, partially cleared space, where the stumps of the trees showed that the wilderness had but lately given way before the advance of man, the battalions were drawn up to see — what?

One solitary man standing in the centre of the circle, with eyes blinded, a target for the bullets of half a dozen bright, glittering rifles fifty yards away.

"I'll not do it," said one. "I came to fight the enemy and not to murder a defenceless man."

"Orders is orders," said another, "and he's a deserter."

"Deserter, indeed! Wouldn't you have done the same in his place?"

"Well, I wasn't in his place, and how do I know what

I would have done if I had been?" with which piece of philosophy he turned away.

The signal given, a flash, a discharge, a muffled scream, and all was over. No one noticed that one of the shots was fired into the air.

General Breckinridge's face grew whiter and whiter as he sat immovable on his horse at the head of his troops and watched the preparations. And when the faint cry was heard he fell to the ground in a dead faint.

What mattered it to the thousands in that camp, who might themselves meet death in the next twenty-four hours, that one soul had gone on before?

When General Breckinridge sought out that once happy little home on the spur of Pine Knob, he found only an empty and deserted cabin. Whether Mary had heard the sad tidings and gone to the settlement in the valley away down below, or whether she had wandered into the wilderness in pursuit of sustenance for herself and little ones, and perished there, no one will ever know.

XXXI

BARTER AND TRADE IN ANDERSONVILLE PRISON

[From Warren Lee Goss's "Jed."]

The teams with rations usually came in at the north gate. These rations consisted of Indian meal, and sometimes of bacon. As a whole there was a large quantity, but when subdivided among twenty or thirty thousand men it gave to each one but a small quantity. A street or path, to which was given the name of Broadway, led from the gate through the stockade from east to west. Here, at ration time, was gathered a motley crowd. With eager, hungry eyes, they watched each division of the food, the sight of which seemed to have a strange fascination for the hungry wretches, long unused to full stomachs. They crowded to the wagons to get a sight of each bag of meal or piece of meat. The attempt to grasp a morsel which sometimes fell from the wagon, the piteous expression of disappointment on their pinched and unwashed faces if they failed, the involuntary exclamations, and the wistful, hungry look, had in them a pathos not easily described.

After the drawing of rations, a dense throng of prisoners always gathered near the north gate to trade. One with tobacco cut in pieces not larger than dice might be seen trying to trade it for rations. Another could be heard crying out, "Who will trade a soup-bone for Indian meal?" "Who'll trade cooked rations for raw?" "Who'll trade beans for wood?" While others with small pieces of dirty bacon an inch or two in size, held on a sharpened stick, would drive a sharp trade with some one whose mouth was watering for its possession. But for its misery, the scene would often have been intensely comical.

The dirty faces, anxious looks, and grotesque garments, and the loud cries, so much in contrast with the usual value of the articles offered, had a humorous side not hard to appreciate even by men as miserable as themselves. The struggle of these thousands, all striving to better their condition by barter and trade, was pathetic. How each bettered his condition by the process of trade, I could never learn.

We had not long been prisoners before we discovered that men here, as in other conditions of life, in order to "get on" and preserve life, must adopt some trade or business. This necessity made men ingenious. Some set up as bakers, and bought flour, and baked biscuits which they sold to such as had money to buy. The ovens which were built showed such ingenuity as to extort expressions of surprise from the Confederates who occasionally visited us. The soil contained a red precipitate of iron, which was very adhesive. This was made into rude bricks by mixing the earth with water, and the oven was built of these over a mould of sand. After being left to harden in the sun for a few days, the sand was removed, a fire was kindled, and the oven was ready for use.

Others made wooden buckets to hold water, whittling out the staves and making the hoops with a jack-knife. Others purchased (of outside parties) sheet tin, generally taken from the roofs of railway cars, and, with a railway spike and a stone for tools, made small camp kettles, without solder, by bending the pieces ingeniously together. These were eagerly purchased by those who had money. As no cooking utensils were possessed by the prisoners, except such as they brought into prison with them, these tinmen were benefactors.

Others tinkered broken-down watches, the object of their owners being simply to make them "go" long enough to effect a trade. The purchaser was usually a Confederate, who found these watch-owners easier to interview before the trade than afterwards, when he

desired to bring them to account for selling watches
that refused to go unless carried by the purchaser.
Others fried flapjacks of Indian meal, and sold them
hot from the griddle for ten cents each. Among the
professional men were brewers, who vended around the
camp beer made of Indian meal soured in water. This
was sold for vinegar, and proclaimed by the venders to
be a cure for scurvy, but was principally used as a re-
freshing drink. A certain enterprising prisoner added
ginger and molasses to the compound, and made, as he
termed his success, a " boom " by selling it. He became
so rich as to buy food, and so regained his health and
strength.

XXXII

BREAD CAST UPON THE WATERS

THE promise is that bread cast upon the waters shall be found after many days. The fulfilment of this promise in its fullest measure was never better exemplified than in the personal history of those who took an active part in the late war. Here are two incidents which show us that the Christian spirit may always be exercised in the midst of commonplace and every-day surroundings.

In 1864, some wounded soldiers lay in a farmhouse in the Shenandoah Valley. Mrs. B——, the mother of one of them, the wife of a neighboring planter, rode ten miles every day to see her boy, bringing with her such little comforts as she could obtain. Her house was burned, and the plantation was in ruins, trampled down by the army. One day she carried to him a pail of beef-tea. Every drop was precious, for it was with great difficulty, and at a high price, that she had obtained the beef from which it was made.

As she sat watching her boy sip the steaming, savory

broth, her eye caught the eager, hungry eye of a man on the next cot.

She turned away with a quick, savage pleasure in his want. He was a Yankee soldier, perhaps one of the very band who had burned her home.

She was a bitter Southerner. But she was also a noble-hearted woman, and a servant of Christ. Her eye stole back to the pale, sunken face, and she remembered the words of her Master, "If thine enemy thirst, give him drink."

After a moment's pause, and with pressed lips, for it required all the moral force she could command for her to do it, she filled a bowl with the broth and put it to his lips, repeating to herself the words, "For His sake; for His sake; for His sake I do it."

Then she brought fresh water and bathed the soldier's face and hands as gently as if he too had been her son. The next day when she returned he was gone, having been exchanged to the North.

Last winter, the son of a senator from one of the Northern States brought home, during the Christmas vacation, as his chum, a young engineer from Virginia. He was the only living son of Mrs. B——, the boy whom she had nursed having been killed during the later years of the war.

She had struggled for years to educate this boy as a civil engineer, and had done it. But without influence he could not obtain a position, and was now supporting himself by copying.

Senator Blank became much interested in the young Virginian, inquired into his qualifications, and after he had returned home used his influence to procure an appointment for him as chief of the staff of engineers employed to construct an important railway. It would yield him a good income for many years.

Senator Blank enclosed the appointment in a letter to Mrs. B——, reminding her of the farmhouse on the Shenandoah, adding, "The wounded man with whom you shared that bowl of broth has long wished to thank you for it. Now he has done it."

A story is also told of two young men, who, shortly before the war broke out, were fellow-students and room-mates at a Pennsylvania college, one a Southerner.

Both were hard students, and aspired to be leaders of their class ; and in time the sharp rivalry between them changed their friendship to bitter enmity. Mutual charges were made, and the hostile feeling finally culminated in a challenge from the Southerner, which the other treated with contempt.

After graduation the young duellist went home, and in the cares and excitements of the following years his college quarrel was forgotten. The memory of it suddenly came back to him one day, after he had become a Christian, and shocked him with the discovery of a surviving hatred.

It was at the battle of Stone River. Our student, now a Confederate officer, was riding across the battle-field, when his horse nearly trod upon a wounded Union soldier. He dismounted, with the humane intention of giving some assistance, but when he looked the soldier in the face, he recognized his old college enemy. He turned quickly to remount his horse, but better thoughts and feelings checked his first cruel impulse, and "in Christ's name" he caused the soldier to be removed to a place of refuge, and procured for him the services of a surgeon and a chaplain.

The wounded man knew his deliverer, but was too weak to utter inquiries or thanks. Informed that his wound was fatal, he could only request that his mother be written to, and assured that he "died like a true soldier;" and this kind service also the Southern officer faithfully performed as soon as the battle was over.

He had no suspicion that the care he had secured for

the sufferer would prove the means of saving his former enemy's life.

After the war, the Northern man wrote to thank his forgiving enemy ; but no answer was received, and further inquiry brought the information that he had been killed.

Twenty-one years passed ; the Northerner was a physician in prosperous practice, when business called him to Charleston, S. C. In a street of that city, then partly in ruins, the two men who had twice been dead to each other met again.

The startled doctor saw the classmate who had once been willing to take his life, and once had saved it. The man had lost his all in the great earthquake ; and his old enemy and grateful friend took him and his needy family back with him to his own city, and established him in a good situation.

XXXIII

THE SURRENDER OF GENERAL LEE

[*From General Grant's "Personal Memoirs."*]

BEFORE stating what took place between General Lee and myself, I will give all there is of the story of the famous apple-tree. Wars produce many stories of fiction, some of which are told until they are believed to be true. The war of the rebellion was no exception to this rule; and the story of the apple-tree is one of those fictions based on a slight foundation of fact. There was an apple

ULYSSES S. GRANT.

orchard on the side of the hill occupied by the Confederate forces. Running diagonally up the hill was a wagon road, which, at one point, ran very

near one of the trees, so that the wheels of vehi-
cles had, on that side, cut off the roots of this tree,
leaving a little embankment. General Babcock, of my
staff, reported to me that when he first met General
Lee he was sitting upon this embankment, with his feet
in the road below and his back resting against the tree.
The story has no other foundation than that. Like
many other stories, it would be very good if it was only
true.

I had known General Lee in the old army, and had
served with him in the Mexican War, but did not suppose, owing to the difference in our age and rank, that
he would remember me ; while I would more naturally
remember him distinctly, because he was the chief of
staff of General Scott in the Mexican War.

When I had left camp that morning I had not expected so soon the result that was then taking place,
and consequently was in rough garb. I was without a
sword, as I usually was when on horseback on the field,
and wore a soldier's blouse for a coat, with the shoulder-
straps of my rank to indicate to the army who I was.
When I went into the house I found General Lee.* We
greeted each other, and after shaking hands took our
seats. I had my staff with me, a good portion of whom
were in the room during the whole of the interview.

What General Lee's feelings were I do not know. As he was a man of much dignity, with an impassible face, it was impossible to say whether he felt inwardly glad that the end had finally come, or felt sad over the result, and was too manly to show it. Whatever his feelings, they were entirely concealed from my observation ; but my own feelings, which had been quite jubilant on the receipt of his letter, were sad and depressed. I felt like anything than rejoicing at the downfall of a foe who had

ROBERT E. LEE.

fought so long and valiantly, and had suffered so much for a cause, though that was, I believe, one of the worst for which a people ever fought, and one for which there was the least excuse. I do not question, however, the sincerity of the great mass of those who were opposed to us. General Lee was dressed in a full uniform which was entirely new, and was wearing a sword of considerable value, very likely the sword which had been presented by the State of Virginia; at all events, it was an entirely different sword from the one that would ordinarily be worn in the field.   In my rough travelling suit, the uniform of a private, with the straps of a lieutenant-general, I must have contrasted very strongly with a man so handsomely dressed, six feet high, and of a faultless form.   But this was not a matter that I thought of until afterwards.

We soon fell into a conversation about old army times.   He remarked that he remembered me very well in the old army; and I told him that as a matter of course I remembered him perfectly.   Our conversation grew so pleasant that I almost forgot the object of our meeting.   General Lee called my attention to the object of our meeting, and said that he had asked for this interview for the purpose of getting from me the terms I proposed to give his army.   I said that I meant merely that his army should lay down their arms, not to take them up again during the war unless duly and properly exchanged.   He said that he had so understood my letter, and that the terms I proposed to give his army ought to be written out.   I then began writing out the terms.   When I put my pen to paper I did not know the first word that I should make use of, I only knew what was in my mind, and that I wished to express it clearly so that there could be no mistaking it. As I wrote on, the thought occurred to me that the officers had their own private horses and effects, which were important to them, but of no value to us : also that it would be unnecessary humiliation to call upon them to deliver their side-arms.

No conversation, not one word, passed between General Lee and myself, either about private property, side-arms, or kindred subjects. When he read over that part of the terms about side-arms, horses, and private property of the officers, he remarked — with some feeling, I thought — that this would have a happy effect upon the army. I then said to him that I thought this would be about the last battle of the war — I sincerely hoped so; and I said further, I took it that most of the men in the ranks were small farmers. The whole country had been so raided by the two armies that it was doubtful whether they would be able to put in a crop to carry themselves and their families through the next winter without the aid of the horses they were then riding. The United States did not want them, and I would therefore instruct the officers I left behind to receive the paroles of his troops to let every man who claimed to own a horse or mule take the animal to his home. Lee remarked again that this would have a happy effect.

The much-talked-of surrendering of Lee's sword and my handing it back, this and much more that has been said about it is the purest romance. The word sword or side-arms was not mentioned by either of us until I wrote it in the terms. General Lee, after all was completed and before taking his leave, remarked that his army was in a very bad condition for want of food, and that they were without forage; and that his men had been living for some days on parched corn exclusively, and that he would have to ask me for rations and forage. I told him "certainly," and asked for how many men he wanted rations. His answer was, "About twenty-five thousand." I authorized him to send his own commissary and quartermaster to Appomattox Station, where he could have all the provisions wanted. Lee and I then separated as cordially as we had met; he returning to his own men, and all went into bivouac for the night at Appomattox.

When the news of the surrender first reached our lines, our men commenced firing a salute of a hundred guns, in honor of the victory. I at once sent word, however, to have it stopped; the Confederates were now our prisoners, and we did not want to exult over their downfall.

XXXIV

THE GRAND REVIEW IN WASHINGTON AT THE CLOSE OF THE WAR

[From General Sherman's "Personal Memoirs."]

By invitation I was on the review stand and witnessed the review of the Army of the Potomac, commanded by General Meade in person. The day was beautiful, and the pageant was superb. Washington was full of strangers, who filled the streets, in holiday dress, and every house was decorated with flags. The army marched by divisions in close column around the Capitol, down Pennsylvania Avenue, past the President and Cabinet, who occupied a large stand prepared for the occasion directly in front of the White House.

During the afternoon and night of May 23, 1865, the Fifteenth, the Seventeenth, and Twentieth Corps crossed Long Bridge, bivouacked in the streets about the Capitol, and the Fourteenth Corps closed up to the bridge. The morning of the 24th was extremely beautiful, and the ground was in splendid order for our review. The streets were filled with people to see the

pageant, armed with bouquets of flowers for their
favorite regiment or heroes, and everything was propi-
tious. Punctually at 9 A.M., the signal gun was fired,
when in person, attended by General Howard and all
my staff, I rode slowly down Pennsylvania Avenue, the
crowds of men, women, and children densely lining the
sidewalks and almost obstructing the way. We were
followed close by General Logan at the head of the Fifteenth Corps. When I reached the Treasury Building
and looked back, the sight was simply magnificent.
The column was compact, and the glittering muskets
looked like a solid mass of steel, moving with the regu-
larity of a pendulum. We passed the Treasury Building, in front of which and of the White House was an
immense throng of people, for whom extensive stands
had been prepared on both sides of the avenue. As I
neared the brick house opposite the lower corner of
Lafayette Square, some one asked me to notice Mr.
Seward, who, still feeble and bandaged for his wounds,
had been removed there that he might behold the troops.
I moved in that direction, and took off my hat to Mr.
Seward, who sat at an upper window. He recognized
the salute, returned it, and then we rode on steadily
past the President, saluting with our swords. All on
his stand arose and acknowledged the salute. Then,

turning into the gate of the Presidential grounds, we
left our horses with orderlies and went upon the stand,
where I found Mrs. Sherman, with her father and son.
Passing them, I shook hands with the President, General Grant, and each member of the Cabinet.   I then
took my post on the left of the President, and for six
hours and a half stood while the army passed in the
order of the Fifteenth, Seventeenth, Twentieth, and
Fourteenth Corps.   It was, in my judgment, the most
magnificent army in existence — sixty-five thousand men
— in splendid physique, who had just completed a
march of nearly two thousand miles in a hostile country, in good drill, and who realized that they were being
closely scrutinized by thousands of their fellow-country-
men and by foreigners.   Division after division passed,
each commander of an army corps or division coming
on the stand during the passage of his command, to be
presented to the President, his Cabinet, and spectators.
The steadiness and firmness of the tread, the careful
dress of the guides, the uniform intervals between the
companies, all eyes directly to the front, and the tat-
tered and bullet-riven flags festooned with flowers, all
attracted universal notice.   Many good people up to
that time had looked upon our Western army as a sort
of mob; but the world then saw and recognized the

fact that it was an army in the proper sense, well organized, well commanded and disciplined; and there was
no wonder that it had swept through the South like a
tornado. For six hours and a half that strong tread of
the Army of the West resounded along Pennsylvania
Avenue; not a soul of that vast crowd of spectators
left his place, and when the rear of the column had
passed by, thousands of the spectators still lingered to
express their sense of confidence in the strength of a
government which could claim such an army.

Some little scenes enlivened the day, and called for
the laughter and cheers of the crowd. Each division
was followed by six ambulances, as a representative of
its baggage train. Some of the division commanders
had added, by way of variety, goats, milch-cows, pack-
mules, whose loads consisted of game-cocks, poultry,
hams, etc., and some of them had the families of freed
slaves along, with the women leading their children.
Each division was preceded by its corps of black pioneers, armed with picks and spades. These marched
abreast in double ranks, keeping perfect dress and step,
and added much to the interest of the occasion. On
the whole, the grand review was a splendid success, and
was a fitting conclusion to the campaign and the war.

XXXV

RUNNING THE BLOCKADE

[From "Debenham's Vow," by Amelia B. Edwards.]

AND now the rapid dusk comes on. The men are at their posts; the captain gives the word; and the Stormy Petrel, which has been busily getting up her steam for the last hour or more, swings slowly round, and works out of the port (Nassau) as composedly and unobtrusively as she had worked in. The chain of lamps along the quays, the scattered lights sparkling along the shores of the bay, the steady fire of the beacon at the mouth of the harbor, fade and diminish and are lost one by one in the distance. For a long time the Stormy Petrel skirts the coast line, keeping in with the Bahamas, and pursuing her way through British waters, but a little after midnight she stands out to sea.

A lovely night, the horizon somewhat hazy after the heat of the day, but the sea breaking all over into phosphorescent smiles and dimples, and the heavens one glowing vault of stars. The Stormy Petrel, her steam being now well up, rushes on with a foam of fire at her bows and a train of molten diamonds in her wake. Thus the night wears, and at gray dawn the boy in the crow's-nest reports a steamer on the starboard quarter.

Scarcely has this danger been seen and avoided than another and another is sighted at some points or other of the horizon. And now swift orders, prompt obedience, eager scrutiny, are the rule of the day, for the vessel is in perilous waters, and her only chance of safety lies in the sharpness of her lookout, and the speed with which she changes her course when any possible enemy appears in sight. All day long, there-fore, she keeps doubling like a hare, sometimes stopping altogether, to let some dangerous-looking stranger pass on ahead; sometimes turning back upon her course, but, thanks to her general invisibility and the vigilance of her pilot, escaping unseen, and even making fair progress in the teeth of every difficulty.

And now the sun goes down, half gold, half crimson, settling into a rim of fog bank on the western horizon. Lower it sinks, and lower, the gold diminishing, the crimson gaining. Now, for a moment, it hangs upon the verge of the waters, and the sky is flushed to the zenith, and every ripple crested with living fire. And now, suddenly it is gone, and before the glow has yet had time to fade, the southern night rushes in.

An hour or so later the wind drops, and the Stormy Petrel steams straight into a light fog which lies across her path like a soft, fleecy, upright wall of cloud.

"This fog is in our favor, Mr. Polter" (the pilot), says Debenham (the supercargo), pacing the deck with rapid steps; for the night has now turned somewhat chill and raw.

"Wa'al, sir, that's as it may be," replies the pilot, cautiously. "The fog helps to hide us; but then, yew see, it likewise helps to run us into danger."

At a little after midnight, when all seems to be solitude and security, and no breath is stirring, and no sound is heard save the rushing of the Stormy Petrel through the placid waters, there suddenly rises up before the eyes of all on board a great, ghostly, shadowy something — a phantom ship, vague, mountainous, terrific, from the midst of which there issues a trumpet-tongued voice, saying, —

"Steamer ahoy! Heave to, or I'll sink you!"

"Guess it's the Roanoke," observed the pilot calmly.

Even as he said the words, the man-of-war loomed out distincter, closer, within pistol shot from deck to deck.

The captain of the Stormy Petrel answered the hostile summons.

"Ay, ay, sir," he shouted through his speaking-trumpet. "We are hove to."

And then he called down the tube to those in the engine-room, " Ease her."

"You won't stop the vessel, Captain Hay?" exclaimed Debenham, breathlessly.

"I have stopped her, sir," snarled the captain.

Then thundered a second mandate from the threatening phantom alongside :

"Lay to for boats."

To which the captain again responded, " Ay, ay, sir!"

Debenham ground his teeth. "But, God of heaven! man," he said, scarcely conscious of his own vehemence, "do you give in thus — without an effort?"

The captain turned upon him with an oath.

"Who says I'm going to give in?" he answered savagely. "Wait till you see me do it, sir!"

And now the Stormy Petrel, her steam being suddenly turned off, had ceased to move. All on the deck stood silent, motionless, waiting with suspended breath. They could hear the captain of the cruiser issuing his rapid orders, trace through the fog the outline of the quarter boats as they were lowered into the water, hear the splash of the oars, the boisterous gayety of the men. . . .

Debenham uttered a suppressed groan, and the perspiration stood in great beads upon his forehead.

"Will you let them board us?" he said hoarsely, pointing to the boats, now half-way between the two vessels.

The captain grinned, put his lips again to the tube, shouted down to the engineer, "Full speed ahead!" and, with one quivering leap, the Stormy Petrel shot out again upon her course, like a greyhound let loose.

"There, Mr. Supercargo," said the captain grimly, "that is my way of giving in. Our friend will hardly desert his boats upon the open sea in such a night as this, even for the fun of capturing a blockade runner."

At this moment, a red flash and a tremendous report declared the prompt resentment of the Federal commander. But almost before those rolling echoes had died away, the Stormy Petrel was half a mile ahead, and not an outline of the cruiser was visible through the fog.

The night passed over without further incident, and by five o'clock next morning the blockade-runner was within eight hours of her destination. Both captain and pilot had calculated on making considerably less

way in the time, and had allowed a much wider margin
for detours and delays, so that now they were not a
little perplexed at finding themselves so near the end of
their journey. To go on was impossible, for they could
only hope to slip through the cordon under cover of the
night. And yet to remain where they were was almost
as bad. However, they had no alternative, so, after
some little consultation, they agreed to lie to for the
present, keeping up their steam meanwhile, and holding
themselves in readiness to repeat the manœuvres of
yesterday whenever any vessel hove in sight.

The fog had now cleared off. The day was brilliant,
the sky one speckless dome of intensest blue. The
blockade-runners would have given much for dark
and cloudy weather. Presently a long black trail of
smoke on the horizon warned them of a steamer in the
offing, whereupon they edged away in the opposite direction as quickly as possible.

Towards sunset the pilot began to look grave.
"Guess we sha'n't know whar we air if this game goes
on much longer," said he. "It aren't in natur not to
get out of one's reck'ning arter dodgin and de-vi-atin'
all day long in this style."

Still there was no help for it. Dodge and deviate the
Stormy Petrel must, if she was to be kept out of harm's

way; and even so, with all her dodging and deviating, it seemed well-nigh miraculous that she should escape observation.

At length, as evening drew on and the sun neared the horizon, preparations were made for the final run. Both captain and pilot, by help of charts, soundings, and so forth, had pretty well satisfied themselves as to their position; and the pilot, knowing at what hour it would be high tide on the bar, had calculated the exact time for going into the harbor.

"'Twouldn't be amiss, cap'n," said this latter, "if you was to change that white weskit for suthin dark; nor if you, sir," turning to Debenham, "was to git quit o' that light suit altogether for the next few hours."

The captain muttered something about "infernal nonsense," but went to his cabin all the same to change the obnoxious garment. Whereupon Mr. Polter gave it as his opinion that if the captain and all on board were to black the whites of their eyes and put their teeth in mourning, it would not be more than the occasion warranted.

The brief twilight being already past, the engineers piled on the coal, the captain gave the word, and the blockade-runner steered straight for Charleston.

And now it is night; clear, but not over-clear,

although the stars are shining. Objects, however, are
discernible at some distance, and ships are sighted con-
tinually. But as none of these lie directly in his path,
and as he knows his own boat to be invisible by night
beyond a certain radius, the captain holds on his course
unhesitatingly. In the mean while, the hours seem to
fly. The Stormy Petrel, now clearing the waters at full
speed, stretches herself like a racer to her work, fling-
ing the spray over her sharp bows and speeding onward
gallantly. About midnight the stars begin to cloud
over and the night thickens ; but there is still no mist
upon the sea. Towards two in the morning the lead
tells that they are nearing shore. Then the pilot gives
orders to " slow down the engines," a breathless silence
prevails, every eye is on the watch, every ear on the
alert, and, momentarily expecting to catch their first
glimpse of the blockading squadron, they steal slowly
and cautiously on their way.

And now the sense of time becomes suddenly reversed. Up to this point the hours have gone by like
minutes ; but now the minutes go by like hours.
Beacons there are none to guide them, for the harbor
lights have all been abolished since the arrival of the
Federal ships outside the bar ; but those on board begin
to ask themselves whether some outline of the coast
ought not, ere this, to be visible.

Still the Stormy Petrel creeps on, still each fresh sounding brings her into shallower water, still those eager watchers stare into the darkness, knowing that the tide will turn and the dawn be drawing on ere long, and that after sunrise neither speed nor skill can save them.

At length, when suspense is sharpened almost to pain there comes into sight a faint, indefinite something which presently resolves itself into the outline of a large vessel lying at anchor with her head to the wind and a faint spark of light at her prow.

The pilot slaps his thigh triumphantly.

"That ar's the senior officer's ship," he whispers. "She lies just tew miles off the mouth o' Charleston bar, an' she's bound, yer see, to show a light to her own cruisers. Zounds, now if we ain't fixed it uncommon tidy this time!"

And now, not one by one, but, as it were, simultaneously, the whole line of blockaders comes into sight, some to the right, some to the left of that which shows the light. Of these they count six besides the flagship, all under way and gliding slowly, almost imperceptibly, to and fro in the darkness.

Between some two of these the blockade-runner must make her final run.

Steam is again got up to the highest pressure, and the Stormy Petrel rushes on at full speed. Then the two ships between which lies her perilous path grow momentarily clearer and nearer, and a dark ridge of coast becomes dimly visible beyond them.

And now the supreme moment is at hand. Straight and fast the vessel flies, her propellers throbbing furiously, like a pulse at high fever, and the water hissing past her bows. Now every man on board holds his breath. Now flagship and cruiser (the one about half a mile to the right, the other about half a mile to the left) lie out a few hundred yards ahead; now, for the briefest second, the Stormy Petrel is in a line with both; now, all at once she is in the midst of a current and rushing straight at that long white ridge of boiling surf which marks the position of the bar !

" By Jove ! " says the captain, drawing a long breath, " we've done it."

" Don't yer make tew sartin, cap'n, till we're over the bar," replies the pilot. " We ain't out o' gunshot range yet awhile."

Over the bar they are, however, ere long, safe and successful.

And now the steam whistle is blown twice, shrill and fearlessly, and two white lights are hung out over the bows of the vessel, for their pilot has been in before, and knows the signals necessary to be observed inside the cordon. Were these signals neglected, they would be fired upon by the Confederate forts.

And now, too, lights are lit, and tongues are loosened, and even the captain unbends for once, promising the men a double allowance of grog. A long irregular line of coast has meanwhile emerged into the gray of dawn; and just as the first flush of crimson streams up the eastern sky, the Stormy Petrel casts anchor under the sand-bag batteries of Morris Island.

XXXVI

BOYS IN THE LATE WAR

[*Gen. Horace Porter in the "Youth's Companion."*]

WHEN a call for troops was made at the outbreak of the war, Young America exhibited himself in his most combative form. Youngsters were the first to enlist, they poured in upon the recruiting officers in swarms like bees ; when too short they strained and stretched to reach the standard of height, and often added a few imaginary years to their lives so as not to be rejected on account of age.

They were afterwards as eager to get at the enemy as they had been to reach the recruiting sergeant, and many a mere lad was much more conspicuous for his bravery than were his elders.

During one of the battles in front of Petersburg, an infantry regiment on a part of the line which had been hard pressed for hours by the enemy began to fall back. The men were becoming more and more demoralized, the color sergeant, who carries the flag in battle, had been killed, the flag had fallen to the ground, and there was serious danger of matters running into a panic.

THE BOY SOLDIER AT THE FRONT.

At this moment, a smooth-faced lad, a mere boy in appearance, snatched up the flag, waved it over his head, cried out to his comrades not to desert their colors, and then with a firm and cheery voice started up the song, " Rally round the flag, boys ! "

As his clear, ringing tones rose above the din of battle, his comrades faced about one after another, caught up the strains of the soldiers' song, and soon the whole line was charging into the enemy with such effect that it swept everything before it, and victory was snatched from defeat.

It seemed the work of inspiration, and the oldest heads in the regiment might have been proud to do the work of the boy who that day had made himself their leader. He was made a sergeant at once for his gallantry.

In an assault on the works which had been constructed around Vicksburg for its defence, a young man belonging to a Western regiment, who seemed to be one of the youngest soldiers in the ranks, pushed ahead with great dash, until he got some distance in advance of the others.

The assault was unsuccessful, and the troops were compelled to fall back. The young man soon found himself left in a Confederate outwork, with about half a dozen of the enemy. Before they could make an effort to take him prisoner he aimed his musket at them and ordered them to file off in the direction of the Union lines.

They were so completely taken aback by the boldness and suddenness of the act, that they offered no effectual resistance, and he triumphantly marched them into camp as prisoners.

The circumstance was reported to the commanding general, and the affair was soon the talk of the camps.

General Grant thought this was the kind of material that should have a permanent place in the army, and he was successful in getting the young man a cadetship at West Point.

His mental capacity seemed to be equal to his courage, and he was graduated from that institution with distinguished honors and given a commission in the Engineer Corps of the army.

Young men have much more to contend against physically in war than their elders. The constitution is not matured, the system is much more susceptible to malarial influences, and they are apt to " break down " sooner under loss of sleep, over-fatigue, inferior food, and the general hardships to which troops must always expect to be subjected during an active campaign.

In the Army of the Cumberland, a little pale-faced
fellow had joined the cavalry, and it is pretty certain
that the recruiting officer who enlisted him had to give
him the benefit of a doubt both as to age and height, in
order that he might come up to the requirements of the
regulations.

He was hardly equal to the work of serving with his
regiment, and was detailed as an "orderly" at headquarters to carry messages or to hold the horses of the
staff officers.

At the battle of Chickamauga, while he was behav-
ing with great coolness, he was struck by a bullet in the
side of the neck. He fell from his horse and was left
on the field for dead.

Twenty years afterwards a gentlemanly-looking man
stepped up to me in a hotel where I was staying, and
asked me if I remembered the little orderly who was
shot at Chickamauga. I said yes, that I recollected the
circumstances of his death very well.

He then turned his head to one side, showed me a
deep groove in his neck, and went on to tell me that he
was the person, that a surgeon had come across him on
the field, had stopped the bleeding, and succeeded in
having him carried to a hospital, that his memory had
left him for two years so that he could scarcely recall

his own name, but he then recovered all his mental powers and became perfectly well.

I found he was a very successful business man, and amongst other enterprises was conducting a large cattle interest in the West. His suddenly turning up in the corridors of a hotel, so many years after his supposed death, seemed like the entrance of an apparition.

The youngest class of enlisted persons in the army were drummer boys. These little fellows suffered a great deal from wounds and still more from disease. The hospitals always contained a large percentage of them, but they were generally cheerful and plucky, and after all showed more endurance than most people would imagine.

They always kept up with the men on the march, though they had to take a good many more steps, and the drum they carried was no small incumbrance in getting over fences and working their way through the tangled undergrowth of forests.

During the battle of the Wilderness, one of these little fellows was seen coming out of the woods with an ugly wound in his arm, and carrying a musket he had evidently secured for the occasion, for drummers do not carry guns.

Going up to a staff officer who was riding to the front,

the boy cried out to him, " I say, colonel, can you tell
me where there's a field hospital ? "

" Right down the road, half a mile in rear," replied
the officer. " You seem to be badly hurt."

"Oh, this ain't nothing ! " said the boy, with the coolness of a veteran. " If I can strike a hospital I'll soon
get this arm fixed up, and come back and have another
crack at the ' Johnnies.' I've been fightin' them now
nigh two years, and I'll just bet you that in that time
I've killed more of 'em than they ever have of me."

Drummers were always handy little fellows on the field.
When they were not required to play with the bands
or beat the "calls," they would help to attend to the
wounded, and carry messages when the men could not
be spared from the ranks for these duties.

While they played a good many pranks, got into no
end of scrapes, and often made life miserable for the
drum-majors whose duty it was to discipline them, they
did many an act that commanded the highest admira-
tion of their officers.

When General Sherman's corps was advancing upon
Jackson, Miss., in the campaign in the rear of Vicksburg, and his troops were engaged in a sharp fight with
the enemy, the general heard a shrill voice calling out to
him that one of the regiments was out of ammunition,

and the men could not hold their position unless a supply of cartridges was sent to them at once.

He looked around and saw that the messenger was a little drummer boy who was limping along the road with the blood running from a wound in his leg.

"All right," said the general, "I'll send the ammunition; but you seem to be badly hurt, and you must go and find a surgeon and get your wound attended to."

The boy started for the rear, and the general was about giving the order for the ammunition, when he heard the same piping voice crying to him, "General, calibre fifty-eight! calibre fifty-eight! Be sure and send them calibre fifty-eight!"

Looking round he saw that the little fellow had turned back and was running after him as fast as the wound in his leg would let him, to describe the kind of ammunition required, which he had forgotten to mention before.

The various regiments were armed with several different sizes of guns. In this one the diameter of the gun barrels was fifty-eight hundredths of an inch, and the ammunition required to fit them was known as calibre fifty-eight.

The general found the boy was more thoughtful than himself, for he had not stopped to inquire of the lad the kind of ammunition needed. He asked the boy his name, complimented him on his coolness and pluck, and promised to remember his services.

The ammunition reached the men, the boy's wound soon healed up, and after the war the general, who has never forgotten the incident, interested himself in the lad's behalf, and procured for him an appointment to the Naval Academy at Annapolis.

Not long ago General Sherman was repeating the story, and the circumstances seemed to be as fresh in his memory as on the day on which the service was performed.

XXXVII

HOW THEY LIVED IN THE SOUTH DURING THE WAR

BEFORE the war, the Southern people were engaged almost exclusively in producing cotton, sugar, molasses, and a few other staple articles, and depended on Europe and the Northern States for manufactured goods. Hence, during the war they felt greatly the need of such articles as cloth, paper, leather, and household utensils. All sorts of ways were devised to supply these.

The wife of a Southern general wrote lately an amusing account of the devices of the Virginian ladies to clothe themselves. Homespun flannel was dyed gray with ivy, purple with maple bark, and green with peach bark. Ball dresses were made of mosquito netting and brocade curtains.

At a time when a pair of boots cost four hundred dollars and a lawn dress two hundred dollars, they grew skilful in making neat gaiters out of bits of cloth and canvas, and in weaving picturesque hats for themselves, their husbands, and brothers, out of corn shucks. Chicken and geese feathers were made, too, into delicate artificial flowers.

Old-fashioned looms were set up, and ladies wove homespun cloth in their homes. Cotton cloths were easily made, but wool was scarce, and the fur of rabbits and other animals was often used instead of it. A lady in South Carolina made very handsome cloths with a warp of cotton and a filling of coon's fur. Leather was difficult to make, so many substitutes for it were devised. It is said that very good shoes were made out of old wool hats, and soft shoes for ladies from squirrel-skins. Wooden shoes were made sometimes, the soles being made of gum wood and the uppers of leather. Soles for boots were made out of saddle-skirts, leather machine-belts, and double thicknesses of heavy cloth with thin pieces of white oak, hickory, or birch bark between them.

Paper was scarce and very costly. Much ingenuity was exercised to find some substitute for it. News-·papers were printed on straw paper and paper hangings. Brown paper and wall paper took the place of ordinary letter paper. Some of the books published at the South during war times are curiosities in the art of book-making.

"There are many little things in which our daily life is changed," said the wife of a Confederate general, "many luxuries cut off from the table which we have forgotten to miss. Our mode of procuring necessaries is very different and far more complicated. The condition of our currency has brought about many curious results; for instance, I have just procured leather, for our negro-shoes, by exchanging tallow for it, of which we had a quantity from some fine beeves, fattened and killed upon the place.

"I am now bargaining with a factory up the country, to exchange pork and lard with them for blocks of yarn to weave negro-clothes; and not only negro-clothing I have woven, I am now dyeing thread to weave homespun for myself and daughters. I have ravelled all the old scraps of fine worsteds and dark silks, to spin thread for gloves for the general and self, which gloves I am to knit. These home-knit gloves and these homespun dresses will look much neater and nicer than you would suppose. My daughters and I being in want of under-garments, I sent a quantity of lard to the Macon factory, and received in return fine unbleached calico — a pound of lard paying for a yard of cloth. They will not sell their cloth for money. This unbleached calico my daughters and self are now making

up for ourselves.   You see some foresight is necessary
to provide for the necessaries of life.

"If I were to describe the cutting and altering of old
things to make new, which now perpetually go on, I
should far outstep the limits of a letter — perhaps I have
done so already — but I thought this sketch would
amuse you, and give you some idea of our Confederate
ways and means of living and doing.   At Christmas I
sent presents to my relatives in Savannah, and instead
of the elegant trifles I used to give at that season, I be-
stowed as follows : several bushels of meal, peas, bacon,
lard, eggs, sausages, soap (home-made), rope, string, and
a coarse basket ! all which articles, I am assured, were
most warmly welcomed, and more acceptable than
jewels and silks would have been.   To all of this we
are so familiarized that we laugh at these changes in
our ways of life, and keep our regrets for graver things."

Before the close of the Civil War the Confederate
currency had depreciated to such an extent that gold
was at more than twelve thousand per cent premium,
and the prices of all articles of trade had risen accord-
ingly.   The situation was similar to that in the colonies
before independence was acknowledged, when it used
to be said : "Before the war we went to market with
the money in our pockets, and brought back our pur-

chases in a basket; now we take the money in the basket, and bring the things home in our pocket."

A Southerner writes of the situation in the Confederacy: "Matters must have been at a pretty pass when quinine sold at two thousand dollars an ounce, and a soldier paid a negro boy two hundred dollars for watching his horse while he ate his dinner."

A cavalry officer, entering a little country store, found there one pair of boots which fitted him. He inquired the price.

"Two hundred dollars," said the merchant.

A five-hundred-dollar bill was offered, but the merchant, having no smaller bills, could not change it.

"Never mind," said the cavalier, "I'll take the boots anyhow. Keep the change; I never let a little matter of three hundred dollars stand in the way of a trade."

Articles raised on the plantations were reasonably cheap. Thus wood could be bought for fifteen dollars a cord, and turkeys sold for ten dollars apiece. Luxuries were very high, and only the richest people could afford them.

Every appeal of the Southern generals to the people for aid was bravely answered by the women of the South. Blankets and overcoats were made for the soldiers at the front from carpets taken up from the floors of hotels and private houses. Beds were stripped of coverings, and rooms of rugs and curtains, and these were duly sent to the suffering soldiers enduring the miseries of a winter campaign in Virginia. Such were the straits and ingenious expedients to which the people of the South were driven during the long and bitter years of the war.

XXXVIII

FOES BECOME FRIENDS

EVEN in the fiercest heat of the war for the Union, Americans did not forget that they were brothers. Veteran soldiers remember it now with more sincerity, because they fought more than a quarter of a century ago for a cause which they deemed the right. Many incidents of individual experiences of the war have been published of late years. The main point in all such incidents is the eagerness with which the kindness of soldiers on the other side is extolled.

There is much in these incidents which may seem sentimental to the generation which was born after the war. But to Americans who remember how mighty were the interests involved in it, and how desperate was the struggle, these signs of the deep cordial peace which now exists between the North and South have a most pathetic and lofty meaning.

Only men who could nobly risk their fortunes and their love for a cause they held to be right could clasp hands when the struggle was over with forgiveness so true and complete.

Let us read of a few such incidents told by veteran soldiers of both sides at the annual reunions.

A private in a New Jersey regiment took part in a skirmish in which he was shot in the ankle, and again by a minie ball under the shoulder-blade, through the right lung. He was left for dead on the field. When he revived, he was surrounded by the Confederates. He lay for hours in an agony of pain and thirst, but summoned courage at last to ask a young lad for a drink.

The boy put his hand on his bayonet, saying, "I would liefer give you this," and passed on. Then suddenly turning, he said, "We are not as bad as you think us," and, stooping, gently lifted the head of the wounded man, and put a canteen to his lips.

A battery was placed near to where he lay, and one of the gunners, a man from Alabama, propped him up on his own blanket, brought a bucket of water and put it within reach, and came to him several times during the night to change his position. The next day a Southern doctor cut off his leg ; he was carried to the hospital in Fredericksburg, and there was nursed by the good women of the town, one of whom he afterwards married.

At the reunion in Gettysburg, a few years ago, of the old soldiers from the North and South, who had fought against each other on that battle-field, many touching little incidents occurred that showed how cordial was the good-feeling now existing between the former enemies.

"Just here," said a crippled New-Yorker, stopping on the corner of a field, "my leg was shot off."

"And just here," said a man beside him, the sleeve of whose gray coat hung empty, "I lost my arm."

The two men became friends at once, pitched a tent on the spot that had been so eventful to both, and there "kept house" together during the whole time of the reunion. Each found the other to be a man of sense, high principle, and good-feeling. They will probably remain friends for life.

So many of the once bitter foes exchanged coats, canteens, and knapsacks, in token of good-will, that it became almost impossible to distinguish Northern from Southern soldiers. They pitched their tents together, most of the men preferring to camp again, instead of going to the hotels, in order that they might meet their old antagonists more freely, and discuss every incident of the battle, about the bivouac fires.

A Northern officer brought to Gettysburg a sword,

gold-handled and set with jewels, which he had taken
from a young Southerner. After the war was over he
had tried in vain to restore it. He now gave it to the
commandant of the corps to which its owner belonged,
in the hope that it might reach him at last.

A large man and a very small one met on the street.

"I think I have seen you before," said the small
man.

" Yes, I took you prisoner," was the reply. Whereupon they shook hands heartily, took dinner together,
and the next day brought a photographer to the spot
where they had fought, and had their pictures taken
standing with uncovered heads and clasped hands.

An old Pennsylvania farmer, after reading an account
of this celebration at Gettysburg, in which both Union
and Confederate soldiers bore a part, said, "I went to
Gettysburg the night after the battle in 1863, and helped
to bury the dead.

"One lad, I remember, in a gray uniform, whom we
dragged from under a heap of dead bodies, was still
breathing. He was but a pretty, chubby-faced schoolboy. We brought the surgeon, and worked with him
for an hour, but it was too late, he was too far gone to
feel the probe. He turned uneasily, smiling and mut-

tering something, which showed that he thought he was back at home.

"'Mother! dear mother!' he said, and tried to lift his arms. Then came the fearful choking, and he was dead.

"Close beside him was the body of a private, belonging to the Sixty-eighth Pennsylvania. He was a young, firmly built man, with a face which, even in death, was gentle and kindly. His sunburned skin and horny hands showed him to have been a farmer.

"In his breast pocket we found a letter from 'Jenny,' with a few words about the crops and the poultry; but the letter was mainly 'Baby,' its doings and sayings, and at the bottom was a great blot made by Baby's own hand.

"Next his heart was a little photograph of a sweet-faced girl and a child, evidently Jenny and the baby.

"We buried the two men side by side.

"The blue and gray coated soldiers, the other day, were talking, and laughing, and fraternizing together over their graves, and near by, the corner-stone of a church, dedicated to the 'Prince of Peace,' was laid.

"But it seemed to me as if those two gallant boys who fought against one another here, each for a cause which he deemed just, must have long ago met elsewhere, and recognized each other as friends, and soldiers under one Captain."

The reception at Atlanta, in the fall of 1881, of the hero of the "March through Georgia," was a striking example of the generosity and warm-hearted forgetfulness of the Southern people. A Southern writer pleads for a better understanding with these people, with whom we were once at war, and draws the following vivid sketch of General Sherman's two visits to Atlanta: —

"He was at Atlanta once — and he looked the city over. I may say he felt it over. He made the acquaintance of its citizens, and its citizens made his acquaintance. The acquaintance may be said to have been mutual if not cordial. It was a decidedly warm acquaintance. When that stern commander got through with the city it looked with its bare and blackened chimneys like a forest of girdlings. Not a building of consequence was left.

"Seventeen years go by, and the man at whose order the city of Atlanta went up in smoke to come down in ashes, is invited by the authorities of the Exposition, a majority of whom were citizens of Atlanta, to return to that city as a guest.

" I said to myself, How will they receive him as they remember their beautiful homes, their business blocks, their churches reduced to ashes, their city which on one day stood fair and beautiful as a bride in the light, and which on the next was a heap of shapeless ruins ?

" I secured my seat early and near the stand in the judges' hall, that I might study the problem of contending emotions, this phenomenon of a people rising superior to their prejudices and even to their very memories. For half an hour the people filed in till the hall was packed. I overheard the conversation which went on about me. One man from Louisville declared it was adding insult to injury — Sherman's return to Atlanta. Two others immediately took him to task. They said to him, —

" 'Do not talk in that way. We live here. Sherman burned our property ; but he did it in the heat of war. While war lasted we fought him ; but the war is over, and General Sherman has come here to-day as the guest of Atlanta.'

" Presently the hero entered with his comrades of the Mexican War, many of them former generals of the Confederate army. Instantly there was an ovation of applause and waving of handkerchiefs. But I said, 'This may be intended for the Southern generals.' The speech was made and the exercises were about to close, when from all parts of the house there arose one universal and prolonged cry of 'Sherman! Sherman! Sherman!' And when he stepped from his place among his comrades and mounted the stand, the applause arose to a deafening roar.

"'I said, 'This is one of the grandest displays of magnanimity to a former foe that the world has ever witnessed.'"

XXXIX

THE BLUE AND THE GRAY

[*Francis Miles Finch.*]

This poem is founded upon an incident that occurred at Columbus, Miss., on Memorial Day, 1867, when flowers were strewn upon the graves of Confederate and Federal soldiers alike.

By the flow of the inland river,
  Whence the fleets of iron have fled,
Where the blades of the grave-grass quiver,
  Asleep are the ranks of the dead;
    Under the sod and the dew,
      Waiting the judgment day;
    Under the one, the Blue;
      Under the other, the Gray.

These, in the robings of glory,
  Those, in the gloom of defeat,
All with the battle-blood gory,
  In the dusk of eternity meet;
    Under the sod and the dew,
      Waiting the judgment day;
    Under the laurel, the Blue;
      Under the willow, the Gray.

From the silence of sorrowful hours
  The desolate mourners go,
Lovingly laden with flowers
  Alike for the friend and the foe;
    Under the sod and the dew,
      Waiting the judgment day;
    Under the roses, the Blue;
      Under the lilies, the Gray.

So, with an equal splendor,
  The morning sun-rays fall,
With a touch impartially tender,
  On the blossoms blooming for all;
    Under the sod and the dew,
      Waiting the judgment day;
    Broidered with gold, the Blue;
      Mellowed with gold, the Gray.

So, when the summer calleth,
  On forest and field of grain,
With an equal murmur falleth
  The cooling drip of the rain;
    Under the sod and the dew,
      Waiting the judgment day;
    Wet with the rain, the Blue;
      Wet with the rain, the Gray.

Sadly, but not with upbraiding,
   The generous deed was done ;
In the storm of the years that are fading,
   No braver battle was won ;
      Under the sod and the dew,
      Waiting the judgment day ;
      Under the blossoms, the Blue ;
      Under the garlands, the Gray.

No more shall the war-cry sever,
   Or the winding rivers be red ;
They banish our anger forever,
   When they laurel the graves of our dead.
      Under the sod and the dew,
      Waiting the judgment day ;
      Love and tears for the Blue ;
      Tears and love for the Gray.

UNION SOLDIERS RALLYING ROUND THE FLAG.

XL

THE BRAVE MEN WHO FOUGHT FOR THE UNION

[*From Gerrish's "Reminiscences of the War."*]

NEARLY a generation has passed away since the breaking out of the war, and many of those now living know
but little of the soldier's sacrifices. These should not
be forgotten; the nation cannot afford to have them
blotted out. They sacrificed for a time all the domestic
relations of life. This may appear to some as a very
small sacrifice to make. But ask that man who, on that
eventful morning, kissed his wife good-by, and pressed
his little child to his breast for the last time, as he
shouldered his knapsack and marched away; or ask the
smooth-faced lad who went forth to battle, with his
mother's kiss damp upon his brow; and they will tell
you of a fearful experience that raged within their hearts.
This is one of the greatest sacrifices that men can be
called upon to make for the country, and none but patriotic men can make it. They sacrificed the conveniences
and comforts of home for the inconveniences and sufferings of the field. No army was ever marshalled

upon the globe, that left such homes of comfort and luxury as did the Union army, in the war of the rebellion. They exchanged the mansion of comfort for the miserable shelter tent ; the soft, clean bed, for a soldier's blanket spread upon the hard ground ; good, wholesome food, for the scanty rations of a soldier ; lives of ease and healthy labor, for the exhaustion and weariness of forced marches ; they threw aside for a period of years the personal liberty so dear to every American citizen, and took upon themselves a species of slavery, to be commanded by other men who were frequently their inferiors in all save military rank. They exchanged a life of comparative safety for one filled with a thousand dangers ; they stepped forth from the peaceful circles of safety, within which so many remained, and boldly stood forth in the way where death passed by ; and there bravely battled for the principles of liberty and justice. All these sacrifices were made for the salvation of the Republic.

These men suffered without complaint. What a lesson may be learned from their example ! I wonder if the young people of our day ever stop to think how much their fathers and grandfathers who fought the battles of the Union suffered, sleeping on the hard, frozen ground, the cold winds sweeping over them, with nothing but their thin, ragged clothing to protect them from the elements, marching barefooted over the rough roads where their tracks were stained with blood that flowed from their lacerated feet, weary and exhausted, famishing with hunger when the government had no bread to give them ; lying for days on the battle-fields between the contending lines, with broken limbs and mangled bodies, the sun pouring its deadly rays upon them, without food, their lips and throats parching with thirst, no medical aid, and their gaping wounds fester-ing in the intense heat.   All this they endured without murmuring, to preserve the Union.   What an example they have set for us to follow !   The patient sufferings of our soldiers through those four years of war should be held up as object lessons before our American youth, for all the years to come, that their hearts may be moulded in the same patriotic love and devotion for the country's welfare.

Our soldiers were brave men, and faced dangers fear-lessly.   The nation, I fear, is forgetting those deeds of bravery too rapidly.   If we could only pass along those battle lines once more, and gather up those feats of in-dividual daring, so many of which occurred in every regiment — deeds, which, if they had been performed in the Spartan wars, or in the days of the Crusaders,

or of Napoleon the First, would have been recorded on
the pages of history, and would thrill the passing gen-
erations as they read! I wish we could gather up the
unwritten history of the war — the deeds that were performed by heroes whose names were never known outside the ranks where they fought, or the beloved circle
of friends at home, and which, if preserved, would fill
volumes. These soldiers were as modest as they were
brave, and many of them have never spoken of the wild
adventures through which they passed, or of the narrow escapes, the hand-to-hand encounters which they
experienced, or of the shot and shells that went tearing past them, so near that the slightest deviation
from their onward course would have caused their
death. These events are locked up within their own
breasts, cherished as sacred reminders of God's providence in preserving their lives. But some evening, as
you sit beside some maimed hero, draw him forth from
his seclusion, get him to unfold that secret chapter of
his life, and as he proceeds with that wonderful narra-
tive, you will decide that I have not exaggerated when I
have claimed that the soldiers who fought for the Union
were brave men.

XLI

MEMORIAL DAY

How dear to the hearts of the American people is Memorial Day, one of the red-letter days of the year. It began in the South. A few mourning women assembled each year to lay flowers on the graves of their dead. The custom soon became general in both South and North. It may be that during the first few years bitterness and animosity towards the living mingled with the honors given to the dead. But sectional enmity faded out of the hearts of both conquerors and conquered long ago. For a few years it seemed as if Decoration Day, as it was first called, would be given over to stump speeches, athletic sports, regattas, and frivolous amusements generally. The sad anniversary of mourning threatened to become a noisy echo of the Fourth of July. The decency and right feeling of the people, however, has checked this tendency, and restored the day to its sacred purpose. With each year, too, the wish has been more widely expressed that not only the graves of soldiers, but of all the heroic dead, should be honored.

How dear to every one, both old and young, are the familiar ceremonies of this sacred anniversary! Year by year, the ranks of the gray-haired and grizzled veterans become thinner as they march on Memorial Day, with faltering steps, in the ranks of the Grand Army of the Republic. The beautiful and pathetic ceremonies of the day are now celebrated in every nook and corner of our broad land. It is exceedingly appropriate that school children should collect the flowers, sing their beautiful songs, and decorate the graves of the heroic dead. It will remind them in the most impressive manner how their fathers and grandfathers fought the battles of their country.

A number of years ago, a famous orator, and a brave officer during the war, was called upon to address the veteran soldiers on Memorial Day in Indianapolis. The following eloquent passage from his oration can be read and re-read many times, and one will not tire of it. Its stirring patriotism is only exceeded by its tender pathos and vivid imagery.

"The past rises before me like a dream. Again we are in the great struggle for national life. We hear the sounds of preparation — the music of the boisterous drums — the silver voices of heroic bugles. We see thousands of assemblages, and hear the appeals of ora-

tors ; we see the pale cheeks of women, and the flushed faces of men ; and in those assemblages we see all the dead whose dust we have covered with flowers. We lose sight of them no more. We are with them when they enlist in the great army of freedom. We see them part from those they love. Some are walking for the last time in quiet woody places with the maidens they adore. We hear the whisperings and the sweet vows of eternal love as they lingeringly part forever. Others are bending over cradles, kissing babies that are asleep. Some are receiving the blessings of old men. Some are parting, who hold them and press them to their hearts again and again, and say nothing; and some are talking with wives, and endeavoring with brave words, spoken in the old tones, to drive from their hearts the awful fear. We see them part. We see the wife standing in the door, with the babe in her arms — standing in the sunlight, sobbing — at the turn of the road a hand waves — she answers by holding high in her loving hands the child. He is gone, and forever.

"We see them all as they march proudly away under the flaunting flags, keeping time to the wild, grand music of war — marching down the streets of the great cities — through the towns and across the prairies —

down to the fields of glory, to do and to die for the
eternal right.

"We go with them one and all.   We are by their side
on all the gory fields, in all the hospitals of pain, on all
the weary marches.   We stand guard with them in the
wild storm and under the quiet stars.   We are with
them in ravines running with blood, in the furrows of
old fields.   We are with them between contending
hosts, unable to move, wild with thirst, the life ebbing
slowly away among the withered leaves.   We see them
pierced by balls and torn with shells in the trenches by
forts, and in the whirlwind of the charge, where men
become iron, with nerves of steel.

"We are with them in the prisons of hatred and famine ; but human speech can never tell what they endured.

"We are at home when the news comes that they are
dead.   We see the maiden in the shadow of her first
sorrow.   We see the silvered head of the old man bowed
with the last grief.

"The past rises before us, and we see four millions of
human beings governed by the lash ; we see them bound
hand and foot ; we hear the strokes of cruel whips ; we
see the hounds tracking women through tangled swamps.
We see babes sold from the breasts of mothers.   Cruelty
unspeakable !   Outrage infinite !

"Four million bodies in chains — four million souls in fetters. All the sacred relations of wife, mother, father, and child, trampled beneath the brutal feet of might. And all this was done under our own beautiful banner of the free.

"The past rises before us. We hear the roar and shriek of the bursting shell. The broken fetters fall. These heroes died. We look. Instead of slaves we see men, and women, and children. The wand of progress touches the auction-block, the slave-pen, the whipping-post, and we see homes and firesides, and school-houses and books, and where all was want and crime and cruelty and fetters, we see the faces of the free.

"These heroes are dead. They died for liberty — they died for us. They are at rest."

XLII

ODE FOR MEMORIAL DAY

BRING flowers to strew again
With fragrant purple rain
Of lilacs, and of roses white and red,
The dwellings of our dead, our glorious dead!
Let the bells ring a solemn funeral chime,
And wild war music bring anew the time
   When they who sleep beneath
   Were full of vigorous breath,
And in their lusty manhood sallied forth,
   Holding in strong right hand
   The fortunes of the land,
The pride and power and safety of the North!
It seems but yesterday
The long and proud array —
But yesterday when even the solid rock
Shook as with earthquake shock, —
As North and South, like two huge icebergs, ground
Against each other with convulsive bound,

And the whole world stood still
To view the mighty war,
And hear the thunderous roar,
While sheeted lightnings wrapped each plain and hill.

Alas ! how few came back
From battle and from wrack !
Alas ! how many lie
Beneath a Southern sky,
Who never heard the fearful fight was done,
And all they fought for won.
Sweeter, I think, their sleep,
More peaceful and more deep,
Could they but know their wounds were not in vain,
Could they but hear the grand triumphal strain,
And see their homes unmarred by hostile tread.
Ah ! let us trust it is so with our dead —
That they the thrilling joy of triumph feel,
And in that joy disdain the foeman's steel.

We mourn for all, but each doth think of one
More precious to the heart than aught beside —
Some father, brother, husband, or some son
Who came not back, or, coming, sank and died :
In him the whole sad list is glorified !
" He fell 'fore Richmond, in the seven long days

When battle raged from morn till blood-dewed eve,
And lies there," one pale widowed mourner says,
And knows not most to triumph or to grieve.
"My boy fell at Fair Oaks," another sighs ;
"And mine at Gettysburg!" his neighbor cries,
And that great name each sad-eyed listener thrills.
I think of one who vanished when the press
Of battle surged along the Wilderness,
And mourned the North upon her thousand hills.
Yes, bring fresh flowers and strew the soldier's grave,
Whether he proudly lies
Beneath our Northern skies,
Or where the Southern palms their branches wave !
Let the bells toll and wild war-music swell,
And for one day the thought of all the past —
Of all those memories vast —
Come back and haunt us with its mighty spell !
Bring flowers, then, once again,
And strew with fragrant rain
Of lilacs, and of roses white and red,
The dwellings of our dead.

SUPPLEMENTARY READING

THE following books will prove of great interest to young people who may wish to read about the great Civil War.

1. C. Carleton Coffin's Days and Nights on the Battlefield.
2. C. Carleton Coffin's Drum-beat of the Nation.
3. C. Carleton Coffin's Marching to Victory.
4. C. Carleton Coffin's Redeeming the Republic.
5. Abbot's Battlefields of '61.
6. Abbot's Blue Jackets of '61.
7. Champlin's Young Folks' History of the War for the Union.
8. Goss's Jed. A Boy's Adventures in the Army.
9. Keiffer's Recollections of a Drummer Boy.
10. Soley's Sailor Boys of '61.
11. Williams's Bullet and Shell.
12. Billings's Hardtack and Coffee.
13. P. C. Headley's Young Folks' Heroes of the Rebellion. 6 volumes: illustrated. Consisting of: Fight it Out on this Line; The Life of General Grant. Facing the Enemy; The Life of General Sherman. Fighting Phil; The Life of General Sheridan. Old Salamander; The Life of Admiral Farragut. The Miner Boy and his Monitor; The Career of John Ericsson, Engineer. Old Stars; The Life of Major-General O. M. Mitchel.
14. Battles and Leaders of the Civil War. 3 volumes, with hundreds of illustrations. Battles and events described by the great generals of the war. An invaluable work of reference for the school library

www.ingramcontent.com/pod-product-compliance
Lightning Source LLC
Chambersburg PA
CBHW030638030726
47497CB00006B/1849